Blue Moon

Also From Skye Warren

Smoke and Mirrors Series
Red Flags
White Lies
Black Sheep

Rochester Series
Private Property
Strict Confidence
Best Kept Secret
Hiding Places

North Security Trilogy & more North brothers
Overture
Concerto
Sonata
Audition
Diamond in the Rough
Silver Lining
Gold Mine
Finale

Endgame Trilogy & more books in Tanglewood
The Pawn
The Knight
The Castle
The King
The Queen
Escort
Survival of the Richest
The Evolution of Man
Mating Theory
The Bishop

For a complete listing of Skye Warren books, visit
www.skyewarren.com/books

Blue Moon

A Smoke and Mirrors Novella

By Skye Warren

1001 DARK NIGHTS
PRESS

Blue Moon
A Smoke and Mirrors Novella
By Skye Warren

1001 Dark Nights
Copyright 2024 Skye Warren
ISBN: 979-8-88542-065-5

Foreword: Copyright 2014 M. J. Rose

Published by 1001 Dark Nights Press, an imprint of Evil Eye Concepts,
Incorporated

Acknowledgments from the Author

Dedicated to the little tan dog in the last chapter, who was created based on my dog who passed away last year. Adventurous, playful, and irrepressibly cheerful. Love you, Tribble.

One Thousand and One Dark Nights

Once upon a time, in the future…

*I was a student fascinated with stories and learning.
I studied philosophy, poetry, history, the occult, and
the art and science of love and magic. I had a vast
library at my father's home and collected thousands
of volumes of fantastic tales.*

*I learned all about ancient races and bygone
times. About myths and legends and dreams of all
people through the millennium. And the more I read
the stronger my imagination grew until I discovered
that I was able to travel into the stories... to actually
become part of them.*

*I wish I could say that I listened to my teacher
and respected my gift, as I ought to have. If I had, I
would not be telling you this tale now.
But I was foolhardy and confused, showing off
with bravery.*

*One afternoon, curious about the myth of the
Arabian Nights, I traveled back to ancient Persia to
see for myself if it was true that every day Shahryar
(Persian: شهریار, "king") married a new virgin, and then
sent yesterday's wife to be beheaded. It was written
and I had read that by the time he met Scheherazade,
the vizier's daughter, he'd killed one thousand
women.*

Something went wrong with my efforts. I arrived in the midst of the story and somehow exchanged places with Scheherazade — a phenomena that had never occurred before and that still to this day, I cannot explain.

Now I am trapped in that ancient past. I have taken on Scheherazade's life and the only way I can protect myself and stay alive is to do what she did to protect herself and stay alive.

Every night the King calls for me and listens as I spin tales. And when the evening ends and dawn breaks, I stop at a point that leaves him breathless and yearning for more. And so the King spares my life for one more day, so that he might hear the rest of my dark tale.

As soon as I finish a story... I begin a new one... like the one that you, dear reader, have before you now.

Chapter One

Luna

My heart slows down in the moments before a performance.

Every second seems to last an hour.

I feel the energy coming off the crowd as they clap and stomp for the tiger who's performing on stage right now. I've seen the same act so many times, so many years of my life that even from backstage, I can see him in my mind standing on his hind feet.

I can see him bouncing a ball.

I can see him jumping through a hoop lit on fire.

There's still a patch of rough skin on his left paw where it caught once during a performance. I can still smell the singed fur and hear the screams of people in the audience.

That won't happen tonight because for the most part, we don't make mistakes.

It's not really professional pride or pleasure at the audience's delight that drives us.

It's my father. He's cruel, merciless.

Mistakes get eliminated, which means they end up rolled into a river somewhere between one town and another as the circus moves along.

So we all learn to do our parts, to play them well.

We learn to smile so hard that no one in the audience ever guesses that we're terrified.

I lean down to stretch my hamstrings, forcing my nose all the way between my legs. When I go out there I need to be limber. But we still have five minutes.

Every drum from the band, every gasp from the audience, they're all choreographed.

They're all a familiar countdown.

One I've played night after night for most of my life.

Maybe for some people the circus is a job.

I've heard distantly that it can even be a dream.

For me, it's only ever been duty.

Duty that I was raised to perform since I was a baby. As a toddler my father taught me to walk on a tightrope. He put down padding when he taught me, but only because bruises are not conducive to performances. I still got them though, bruises. I fell so many times that the bruises started forming on my feet. My skin would crack open and my father would pick me back up and put me on the tightrope even as blood dripped down onto the mats. That's how I learned balance.

After stretching forward, I stand up straight and then lean backwards and backwards and backwards. Flexibility. Sometimes people come up to me after a show and marvel over how my body is so flexible. Am I double-jointed? they ask. Was I just built this way? No. My body started off like everyone else's, but I pushed harder than I should have, harder than is safe, and even then my father stepped in and pushed harder.

Flexibility was the only way that I could escape the injury he inflicted on me.

So I learned it.

Standing with my feet planted firmly on the ground, I bend backwards until I can reach my ankles, then I come back up again and freeze because someone is there—a man.

He has dark hair, a little glossy with a surprising amount of volume.

One part falls rakishly over his eye.

Dashing, that's the word that comes to mind.

He looks dashing.

Which I distrust immediately.

Dashing isn't real, it's a fairy tale.

And I learned a long time ago that fairy tales don't exist.

The twinkle of mischief in his eyes proves me right. The fact that he's tall with broad shoulders, obviously strong, even through his suit, that doesn't matter. None of it matters.

He's a stranger and even worse, a townie.

Circus folk are insular, almost xenophobic.

We take money from the people in town. We serve them popcorn and we perform for them, but we never trust them. He is some member of the audience who decided to sneak backstage for reasons unknown. Probably so he could hit on the performers.

It'll be a lucky thing if my father doesn't see him.

Underperforming circus folk aren't the only people he's ever rolled into a ditch as the caravan moved through a lone moonlit highway.

The man leans back against a temporary wooden wall.

"Like what you see?" he asks.

My cheeks flush, I've been staring like an idiot. "You shouldn't be back here."

He looks around. "I don't see a sign."

"There doesn't need to be a sign. This is backstage. You should be in the stands."

"No," he says, "I should be in neither of those places. I belong in the ring."

I roll my eyes at the arrogant statement, even though it rings true.

This is a man who would be perfect as a performer. He commands attention just by standing there. He's commanding my attention right now.

"Go ahead." I tell him, "Sasha probably wants a snack."

Something dark flashes across his eyes. "She probably does. That's what you do to the animals, right? You keep them hungry before a performance. Of course, you don't want to go too far. You don't want them *too* hungry. You don't want them to decide that one of the audience members looks more delicious than whatever the trainer's got on a stick."

I shiver. "You don't know anything about us."

"Don't I?" He pushes away from the wall and walks toward me.

I want to back away, but I force myself to stand my ground.

I belong here, he doesn't.

Besides, I can't miss my cue. I don't think my father would actually push me into a ditch, but that's not because of familial love. I'm the headliner for the circus right now. The draw.

The reason why we get even tiny snippets of media in local TV shows when we pass through towns. The great Luna Rider, so much potential, Olympic hopeful...

At least she was a long time ago.

Now she's just a circus sideshow, something to do on an afternoon in a rural town.

The stranger circles me, watching far too close for comfort, his dark eyes taking in everything from my hair in its tight bun to my leotard, my stockings and my bare feet. And they aren't pretty feet. They're the feet of a dancer, of an athlete. They're feet that were cut time after time on tight ropes when I was just little.

The audience can't see them, so it doesn't matter that I can't cover them up with ballet shoes or something else in order to do my act.

This man sees them.

He seems to notice every cut and bump and scar.

He meets my eyes. "I do know you," he says, his voice low, so low.

I almost don't notice how close he is. Not until his breath brushes my temple, warm and almost soothing. In contrast to his words.

"I see that they keep *you* a little hungry too. That you're strong, muscular, but not as much as you should be. Not for someone who works out ten hours a day. That's because they keep you hungry, isn't it? You wake up hungry, you perform hungry, and you go to sleep hungry."

A full body shiver racks me, confirming his words even as I want to deny them.

Yes. My father trained me the same way he trained the animals.

And the worst part, the reason why I can't even condemn him, is that it works. He wanted to build something to revive his flailing circus.

He worked at it and now he has it.

I remember when we would only draw a handful of people when I was a child. They were more concerned with drinking and fighting in the stands than watching the show.

Now, our biggest tent packs 100 people a night, even more if my father can sell the tickets, the fire marshal's rules be damned.

"I'm serious," I say, my voice unsteady. "You shouldn't be back here. The owner of the circus will be upset if he finds you."

"And then what?" he says. "Will he kick me out of the circus? No refunds, right?"

"Right."

"Is that what you want?" He circles me again. And from behind, he leans down, his words soft, his lips moving against my neck. My entire body wakes up, that's the only way to explain it. It comes alive. After nineteen years of sleep, I thought my body was only good for one thing—performing, doing what other people want to see. But this reaction that runs through me, it has nothing to do with being seen. It has to do with feeling the warmth of him behind me, the strength and size of him. A contrast to the softness of his mouth.

He kisses his way up toward my ear.

I should be offended.

I should be horrified.

I should turn around and slap him.

Except then everyone would hear us.

The audience might look over.

The show would stop.

My father would definitely find out.

So I stand very still.

At least, that's the excuse I give myself as I allow his teeth to gently grab my earlobe and tug. It feels like there's a direct path to between my legs.

My nipples turn hard, visible beneath the leotard.

They're barely there, my breasts.

I didn't develop much when I went into puberty. I've always been relatively flat, which served me well when it comes to acrobatics. It's almost like I haven't had breasts until right now, until this moment, when suddenly they've decided to make themselves known. And I want nothing more than for his long-fingered, elegant, masculine hands to be on them.

"What are you doing?" I ask.

"Introducing myself," he murmurs. "It's so very nice to meet you."

The audience laughs, reminding me that I need to be on stage in about 30 seconds.

It's almost my cue.

There's no stage director back here to point it out. I'm just supposed to know, and I always do. No stage director, which means there's no one to see when his hand comes around, splays over my stomach and tugs me back so I can feel him hard and thick against my ass.

"I think I'm going to be seeing a lot of you, Luna Rider," he whispers.

I whirl to face him. "No, you're not."

"I am if you accept my job offer."

An offer of sex. In exchange for things. Money. A car, maybe. Men like him have money. You can tell from his clothes. His confidence. My cheeks flush, because I liked him touching me a little too much. When I thought he wanted me. When I thought he *saw* me, not a body he could purchase as easily as a ticket on the tilt-a-whirl. "No, thanks."

"You don't even want to hear it?" he asks.

"There is *nothing* you could say that could tempt me."

"I don't know," he muses. "I've said so many alluring things."

"Please leave." Agitation makes me twitch. "*Leave.*"

And then, miraculously, he does.

He turns and walks away.

Thank God, I tell myself, pretending I'm glad the alluring stranger is gone.

He can only cause trouble.

Nothing good ever comes from strangers or townies or men for that matter.

I look down.

My nipples are still hard. There's still a warmth and maybe even a slight dampness between my legs. How is it possible that someone could do that in only a few minutes? What is his name? How did he know mine? Maybe he's some kind of Olympics superfan.

He saw an article or a blog post on the local news station and decided to come say hello in a very inappropriate way. With a proposition. An offer of money for sex.

Well, if that's the case, it should be over soon.

It should be over now.

As long as he doesn't go to my father next. I shiver again, and this time it's desire tinged with fear. Somehow that only makes me hotter.

I hear the announcer boom over the speakers indicating that Sasha the beautiful orange-and-black striped tiger is off the stage, along with the rest of the animals and the handler. "And now the amazing Luna Rider soars through the air. Give her a glorious welcome."

I snap into action and run as fast as I can. With every beat of my heart, I run.

There's a trapeze waiting for me down low, reachable. It only takes a small hop, and then I'm on it soaring, soaring through the air, allowing myself to turn and tumble, falling and catching, falling and catching.

This is the one place where I control what happens.

This is the only place in my life where I'm free.

Chapter Two

Emerson

Unconventional, that's how I would describe my recruiting style.

Logan Whitmere, the owner of Cirque des Miroirs, would probably have other words for it, but he's not here. He wants to stay with the circus where his wife performs each night. He used to do all the traveling. Talent is serious business in the circus world. The best acrobats get poached from circus to circus.

It's a competitive industry and our circus is at the top, at least it is right now.

In order to stay that way, we always need to be looking for fresh shows, fresh performers. A lot of athletes who have the skill would rather settle down at a show that's stationary.

Our circus moves around, so we need someone who's both great and flexible in more ways than one. Luna Rider fits the bill.

There's only one tiny little problem where she's concerned.

Her father.

It's an open secret in the circus world what happened to Luna Rider, how she was scouted for the U.S. Olympic Gymnastics Team before she was even old enough to join the team.

They groomed her for a spot there. Years and years of practice, dedication, skill. It could have led to an entire career. She could have been a household name. And then one day… she stopped. A fall, the rumors speculated. An injury that would preclude her from being at the top. Perhaps, but details never came out. All of those dreams dashed.

Her father owns this circus. He is not precisely known for his geniality, which is especially ridiculous when you consider that he's also the ringmaster. Sometimes people do both jobs, but it means they're not doing them both very well.

As the owner of Cirque des Miroirs, Logan plans.

He makes sure that our show is always sharp, that we're bringing in good money, that we're taking care of everything that needs to be taken care of.

Meanwhile, the inside of the ring, that's my domain.

That's where I rule.

Based on the shoddy condition of the tent and the lean look of the animals, they're not making good profits at Blue Moon Circus.

Enthusiastic clapping rises when Luna Rider's name is called. It's like a flip was switched inside her. One minute she's a melty, aroused, beautiful little body waiting for me to command, and the next minute she's an athlete. No, more than that. An athlete is still a person, and she stopped being that.

She became something else instead, an animal, something that can fly, that can soar through the air, defying gravity. That's the irony of these performances. People come expecting to be surprised, expecting to be impressed.

The bar is already fucking high, and she flew past it.

She has everyone exclaiming, clapping, crying out, cheering for her.

Every person in the stands holds their breath, roots for her.

I stand backstage and watch her soar through the air, my heart in my throat. She's a goddamn professional. That's why I'm here, to scout her, and yet there's a knot in my throat when she does the triple somersault.

Most of her flips rely on her arm strength, something I recognize because I've seen enough acts like this. There's one part where she catches herself by her feet, her toes pulled back, forming a little hook that she uses to swing on the wooden bar.

I wince, knowing how excruciating that would be for someone to hold their body weight that way as inertia pulls them away. It would hurt for anyone, but for someone nursing an old injury, brutal. If she were mine, I wouldn't let her do that trick.

There are others just as impressive that she can do without having to hurt herself every night. She's not mine, but that's going to change.

I watch the rest of the show, my fist clenched around a board near me, my knuckles white. Her skill is undeniable, as is her passion, her talent. There's almost an otherworldly ability of hers to fly through the air as if gravity doesn't apply to her. But I also see all of the danger, all of the risk, the way her entire routine is based on doing the most dangerous stunts back-to-back, again and again. I notice the way the net underneath her doesn't look new or very well secured. There are no spotters. I doubt there's even a medic on staff, no one to help if she went tumbling twenty, thirty feet to the ground.

I'm going to own her.

I decide it right there and then, as the crowd practically swoons at what looks like a near miss but is actually perfect execution. I'm going to own her for more than just Cirque des Miroirs's new act.

She's going to be mine in every sense of the word—under me, around me.

I'm going to know every nuance of her skin, every bruise and scar, every muscle that twitches. I watch through the end of the show until her solo act is finished.

This is when she should be finished.

She's already expended more energy.

Anything she does now will just increase the likelihood that something will go wrong. That she'll get injured. Instead, she has to change her costume quickly and become part of the group act because this circus doesn't have enough people.

I skip the group act and go in search of my prey.

In this case, it's Luna's father.

Everything is a shade more dingy, more dirty, more dark in this circus, but I still recognize the feel of it, the flow. I can still see the difference between the brightly lit fairgrounds and the private area where performers take their breaks, where operators rest between shows.

There should probably be security somewhere around here, at least minimal security, but there isn't, no one to stop me as I wander through the tired-looking RVs.

A woman holding a baby looks at me, her eyes wide, her lips pursed. She doesn't try to stop me, nor does she call for help. This is a woman who knows that there is no one to help. "Michael Rider," I say, reaching back to hold up a hundred-dollar bill.

Her eyes glance toward a particularly large RV.

"Thank you," I say, handing it over.

This is the evening show, the one that comes after the matinee, which means dusk has already settled over the cold Oregon terrain. I give a hard knock. Someone shirtless and sweaty opens the door, looking as though he's expecting someone else.

He frowns. "Who the hell are you?"

"A customer," I tell him. "Looking for Mr. Rider."

He squints his eyes, clearly too young to be my prey, "Mr. Rider ain't looking for you."

"Nevertheless, I think he will want to hear my offer." There's a shout from inside, which distracts the younger man in front of me. I push past him.

Then I'm inside an RV that has definitely seen better days.

The cupboards have been rotted from water damage. There's a smell of mildew in the air. Five men are gathered around a table playing poker, playing poker in the middle of a circus with a show going on, which is absolutely a fucking scandal. This many able-bodied men sitting around in the middle of a goddamn show?

Logan would never allow this.

It's clear from the way they're sitting who's in charge here.

He has his back in the corner so he can see everyone at all times. This is someone who doesn't trust people, even the ones who are closest to him.

I would know this based on where he's sitting and based on the look of boredom on his face, even if I didn't recognize the same features in his daughter.

It's the eyes really.

This man's face is large with jowls and whiskers, completely unlike the delicate, ethereal beauty who's working inside the tent, earning the money that he's using to gamble away right now with plastic chips and bent, most likely marked, cards.

Their eyes are the same though, a wintry gray.

On her, it makes her look a little bit like a fairy.

On him, it makes him look like a cold half-dead bastard. "Who the hell are you?" he asks.

"Emerson Durand."

"Get the fuck out of here."

"Ah, I see my reputation precedes me. That will save us time."

"We don't want your kind around here."

"My kind. Do you mean the French? I don't think we've done anything especially offensive recently. Then again… notre existence même offense les hommes ordinaires, qui ne peuvent jamais être à la hauteur."

He snarls. "Speak in English, damn you."

The other men are watching with barely suppressed violence. They're just waiting for his cue so they can attack. Unfortunately, their bloodlust will not be satisfied today. There's far too much record of me coming here for them to dispose of my body quietly.

"Then again, perhaps you are talking about my kind as in ringmasters. That's what you are, isn't it? You are listed as the official ringmaster of this circus. And yet we heard a recording in the tent. Is it perhaps that you're feeling under the weather?" I look around, obnoxiously exaggerating, taking in the cards and the bottles of beer and the haphazard stack of empty pizza boxes. "No, that can't be it. Were you training someone?"

"Townies can't tell the fucking difference. I say the same damn thing every night."

I make a tsking sound. "And your daughter performs the same tricks every night. Should she just put up a recording? Perhaps you can drop a large projector screen to show the audience."

He stands up. "You got a purpose here? I know about Whitmere. I know what he's done."

"That could mean a lot of things."

Michael Rider isn't the only one who metes out his own form of justice.

Circus people learn early not to trust law enforcement. We take care of things our own way. And when Logan met Sienna, the woman he's now married to, she was in a bad situation.

He fixed that for her in a very permanent sense, a very felony sense.

Somehow I don't think Michael Rider knows anything about that or particularly cares.

"What part exactly?" I ask.

"How he poaches performers from other shows, makes it harder for us to keep going, how he pays them extra and gives them health insurance."

"Ah, that." It's actually one of the least offensive things Logan Whitmere has done, but, naturally, this man wouldn't see it that way.

"You're not taking her," he says. "I know who you want."

He knows because she's the only talent this circus has.

I'm not going to say that out loud because I don't trust these assholes to realize people probably know that I'm here. They could definitely attack like a pack of hyenas and think about the consequences later.

The gun I'm packing might or might not get me out of that scrape, but I'd rather not test that theory. "Gentlemen, I can see how hard you work."

I hope that my sarcasm doesn't shine through, as I study the collection of chips piled into the middle of the table, while everyone else does the work that actually runs the circus.

I know it doesn't because I'm a damn good ringmaster.

I don't allow recordings of my voice to run the circus.

No, I do it myself. And I have the audience in my thrall every single night.

I have them in my thrall tonight, even though my audience is a handful of bastards in another circus. "And I'm telling you, I can change all of that. I can make your lives infinitely easier. You see, the amount of money that Logan Whitmere and our circus are willing to pay to acquire new talent is so obscene, so gargantuan, that you gentlemen here might never have to work again. Think of it. The same amount of money you would make night after night, traveling the country, but you would have it in your hands right now."

A couple of men exchange glances. They're looking for the easy way out. This is the easiest way out. I can see that I've pulled half of them over to my side.

Only, Rider doesn't look convinced, not even a little bit.

That's not particularly surprising. He's slow and cruel, but he's not stupid.

He knows that if he were to get a windfall, first of all, he wouldn't share it with any of these men. Second of all, he knows how quickly he would spend and lose the money. This is not a man who's known for winning.

The only thing he has, the only thing he's ever had of value is his daughter.

I see it in his gray eyes, those eyes that are so like Luna's.

He's not going to give her up, not for any amount of money.

It's possible there's more to it than just dollars, though I wouldn't actually claim any sort of familial bond. After all, if he actually cared about her, he would've let her win the Olympics and change her fucking life. Possession, control, those are the things that drive this man, which means he's not going to give it up.

"Get the fuck out of here, Emerson Durand," he says with a snarl. He takes a swig of beer and slams the bottle back down. "We don't want your money."

"Are you sure? I think that one there, he would like my money." I point to a man with the tallest pile of chips seated at the table, the winner, though it's not very much of a high bar in this group. "What do you say?" I ask him.

He leans forward, choosing his words carefully. Highest IQ in the room, that's what would be my guess. But again, not a high bar. "I say we should hear out the offer," he says, looking sideways at Rider. "What could it hurt to know the details?"

Rider snarls. "This man is nothing but flash. Nothing but talk. You see the way he talks to us like we're some idiot townies sitting in the stands of his circus. It's bullshit."

"I want to hear it," says another man, emboldened by the first. He's got no chips in front of him. An absolute idiot, but at this point, I'll take all the help I can get.

"Maybe it'll be worth it," I say, sounding fatigued at just the idea. "Setting up every night, tearing down every night, it wears on a man."

Rider shakes his head. "No."

I wonder how much Luna's refusal to accept my offer was rooted in this, knowing her father would never let her go. She's a grown woman, an adult, but the circus, it operates with different rules, old-fashioned rules where the man is the head of the household and where the owner of the circus, he runs everything.

Generally speaking, he would have to agree to allow one of his talent to go.

Most talent sign contracts, though looking around this place, I doubt they bother with such formalities. Contracts are just words after all, and these men look like they would hold her to a promise she made when she was two years old under threat of violence.

"How about a different approach?" I say, pulling out one of the empty seats and sitting down. At least the other men at the table, the ones who actually want my money, allow me to sit without shoving me out the door.

An angry flush blooms on Rider's ruddy cheeks. "You already have my answer."

"I'm not making another offer," I say in a soothing tone. "Don't worry. Instead, I'm placing a stake." I reach into my pocket, inside my jacket, and pull out a checkbook.

I write down a number that has a bunch of zeros, tear it off and place it at the center of the table on a pile of chips.

"This should buy my entry, don't you think?"

Considering they were probably playing for $5 and $10 chips, this is more than the entire pot. "There's more where that came from. Ten times as much if you win. Then again, if I win…"

"We're not fucking playing," Rider says.

The man with the most amount of chips snarls. "It's just an entry fee," he says to Rider under his breath. "I can win. I can get it."

"And what if you don't?" Rider snaps. "She's the reason anyone sits in those seats. She's the reason we sell a single fucking ticket. Half the rides don't work," he says, not caring in this room if he derides his own circus. "The games just steal their money without even pretending to provide any fun. She's the only reason this circus runs."

Then why do you treat her like shit?

That's what I want to ask, but I don't. I keep my mouth shut as the other men argue in favor of playing the game, playing the game because it's five against one.

If a single one of them wins, they get to keep the money.

"Come. Gentlemen, I'm sure you can see reason. I'm only one man. What are the odds that I would win?" Rider doesn't particularly like my odds either, but he knows what's at risk.

They're also going to cheat within an inch of their lives, but that's okay.

I can cheat too.

See, I'm much more like these men here than the ones back at my own circus.

I understand deception, violence. I understand the cold, dark drive to achieve perfection, to do what's right for me at the expense of everyone else.

Yes, I understand them.

I'm one of them.

I belong here more than I do at my circus, but that's not going to stop me.

Rider's eyes, those gray familiar eyes are focused on the check and all the many zeros. "Fine," he says. "Five games, whoever has the most at the end wins."

"Just to clarify. If I were to win, in that unlikely event, I would get Luna."

Rider growls. "It's not going to happen."

"Right, but if it did."

"Yes," says the man with the highest amount of chips, his voice smooth. "And if any one of us wins, then we get another check that's ten times this amount. Deal?"

"Deal." I pull out my phone. "You heard all that, right?"

My friend on the other end says, "Yep, got it."

"It's not that I don't trust you, gentlemen," I tell them somewhat apologetically. "It's just that I don't trust anyone. You are unfortunately part of anyone."

I end the call and shove the phone back in my pocket.

It's a little insurance policy so I don't end up dead tonight. Though that's still a possibility and the calculated risk adds a piquant note of sweetness to an otherwise dull affair.

Reckless, that's what Whitmere would call my approach to recruiting.

Good thing he's not here.

Without a word they allow the man with the most amount of chips to deal, which means they all tacitly know he cheats, and of course he does. I watch as he carefully slides cards out from the top and a few from the bottom as he deals.

Predictably, I lose the first round.

I would have lost anyways even without the cheating, but it was handy. It was handy to see them gloat. It was handy to find out their tells.

By the third game we're even.

And by the fifth when my hand is full of clubs and he lays down his three-of-a-kind, I've won the game. I've won the pot. I've won the best trapeze artist in the country. Luna Rider is mine. Now let's see if we can leave the fairgrounds alive.

Chapter Three

Luna

News travels fast in the circus.

I hear about it first via text.

One of our rigging guys quit last week and there's no money to get a replacement nor would anyone want to accept a job from Blue Moon Circus. Seeing as how my father verbally and occasionally physically berates people for their mistakes. All of which means that when we got to the big elephant act, I am the one managing the lights.

My phone vibrates. I check it because if anything goes wrong in the circus, I'm usually the first one to know. The first one to know before my father knows, that way I can manage him if I need to. Not that I'm always successful at managing him, but at least I try.

The first text just says *SOS*, and I know in my very heart that it has to do with that guy.

He probably went to go see my dad.

An argument ensued and someone is dead. We're lucky if the cops don't get called. I don't know what to do about that, seeing as I'm currently managing a spotlight on Dumbo.

Yes, we stole the name from the Disney show and they do not care because we are just a speck of dust. Dumbo is a tired, old elephant. She should have been retired to a sanctuary years ago, but instead she has to keep working, standing on her arthritic back legs for the oohs and aahs of the audience.

The next time I hear something is after the show. Freddy, who works in concessions, runs up to me and tells me about the news. It's apparently spreading like wildfire.

And it's even worse than an argument.

There was an agreement made, an agreement that I'm going to go work for a different circus. That can't be right. I tell him that, and he shrugs knowing that it can't be right, but that's the news. I'm still busy helping everyone file out of the tent in a safe and somewhat orderly manner so that we can begin tearing it down because we're moving to another city tomorrow.

My father would wait until the last minute.

He would wait until tomorrow morning and then yell at everyone for it not being done. So I learned early on to get everyone together so we could do the job when it needed to be done, which is tonight, even though we're all tired, we all pitch in, including me.

It doesn't matter that I'm a performer or that my name is on the posters or that I have to sign autographs after the show, smiling for the little kids and listening to the little girls who tell me about their gymnastics. That's the highlight of my day, actually, but when all of that is over, I have to help tear down the tent and pack everything away so we can go to the next city. We're done around midnight and that's when I would normally head back to my trailer, but I need to find out what's going on so I head straight to my father's trailer instead.

It's a place I tend to avoid when I can, but this is unavoidable.

I knock on the door. I expect Joe to answer it since he's my father's unofficial butler. That's my inside joke by the way. He's my father's unofficial everything, but mostly he's my father's muscle. He's delivered slaps to me when my father was too drunk and too angry to bother to do it himself.

Instead, the person who opens it is none other than the stranger from earlier.

He is surprisingly not black and blue, not beaten to bits. In fact, he looks healthy and haughty. His dark eyes twinkle like he has a secret with me. "Luna," he says as if we're old friends, which is not a good thing. It's just another reason for my father to hate me later. Because whatever happens between this man and I, whether it's sexual or not, dangerous or not, there's no way I'm leaving Blue Moon Circus. "Come on in."

I step cautiously into the room.

I've stepped foot into this trailer thousands of times, maybe millions of times, I don't even know. This was my family home, my childhood home, if the word home could be applied to such a place of terror. But the scene is unlike anything I've ever seen before.

Instead of my father's poker game or a few of the female performers passed out on his lumpy couch for him to use whenever he wants, there are two men I don't recognize with guns. Pointing them at my father and a couple of his buddies who usually play poker with him.

Chips are scattered all around the room.

The card table is upended. Something bad happened here though you couldn't tell by looking at Emerson, he smiles. "We had a slight disagreement at the end of our card game. However, the results stand. I won, which means that you come with me."

Horror arises inside me along with outrage. The outrage is easy. "What the hell are you talking about? I can't be won in a card game. I am a human."

"Anything can be won," he says, "just like anything can be gambled away, and that's what your father did. He gambled you away."

I look to my father who already has an eye that's starting to swell and turn black, which means he got into a fight. This is not a huge surprise. He gambles things. He loses, then he fights and he normally wins those fights because he mostly just gambles with people who are in his circus and, ultimately, he's the boss.

This time he didn't win.

He lost and he gambled more than a few thousand dollars.

He gambled me.

I'm surprised by the sense of loss in my chest, by the hollowness there. It shouldn't be possible for my father to disappoint me anymore. He's done it enough times. I know there's no real love between us. We've never hugged or said, "I love you." We never had father-daughter moments. The first time I got my period, I cried because I didn't know what it was.

It was Julie, the costume designer, who taught me how to use tampons.

We don't really have a relationship, but it still hurts to know that he was willing to gamble me, a person, a human, his daughter in a poker game.

"Why?" I ask, the question falling from my lips unbidden.

He snarls, "You're no longer useful to me, girl. Go ahead and go then. Go with this man to some fancy circus where they're probably going to make you spread your legs for the highest paying VIP ticket holder, see if I care."

I flinch because that's exactly what he has made me do. "I'm not leaving," I whisper.

It's not because I'm loyal to this place. There's something deeper that binds me here, something that neither of these men know or care about. It's love.

"I hate to contradict a lady," Emerson says, "but in this case I must. You are indeed coming with me. It's a binding contract."

I scoff, "Show me where the signature is."

He gives me a derisive look. "You know how the circus works. What's on paper doesn't matter. The only thing that matters is your word, and in this case you were owned by your father. He decided to play a game and lost, now you belong to me."

I bare my teeth at him. "I belong to no one."

He grins. "This will be fun."

I turn to leave, but one of the armed men stands in front of the door. He doesn't look me in the eye, instead he looks a few inches up and a few inches to the right as if I'm anonymous, as if I'm anyone that he's holding captive, armed and dangerous and muscular as he stands blocking my exit.

Emerson makes what sounds like a regretful noise in his throat. "I do not wish to alarm you, mademoiselle, but expediency is of utmost importance. I would not want a small circus uprising to turn dangerous for anyone in this room. It's best that we leave quickly. You'll become accustomed to your fate. You may even grow to like it."

He's talking about performing for a circus, and frankly, I might have liked performing for another circus if it weren't for the little girl a few trailers over.

That's not what he means though.

There's a purr in the way he speaks, an insinuation that he's talking about more than performing for the circus. When he says that I might even come to enjoy it, he's talking about himself, about sex, which is definitely not happening.

I'm not leaving.

I'm not performing for another circus.

And I'm definitely not ever—100% sure—having sex with Emerson Durand.

I turn to face him. "Can I speak with you outside where there aren't any guns?"

"Of course, mon amie," he says, leading the way outside.

I take a deep breath of the frigid air and it centers me. This is what I'm used to, cold, loneliness, fear. I've survived all those other times, which means I can survive this.

"Cut the act," I tell him.

He raises his eyebrows in question.

"Listen, I know how it works," I say, "I know that you have to pretend to be all macho and bullshit around the other guys to get any respect. I've been in the circus my whole life."

He grins, "You see right through me, is that it?"

"Yes," I say, "I see right through your bluster and I know you aren't going to force a woman into your circus and into your bed just because you won some stupid poker game."

"You know all that about me? From what, from how I look?"

No, I can't agree with him there. He looks like a modern-day pirate, like he would easily plunder a ship, a town, like he would take whatever he wants. And right now, the way he's looking at me, the way he scans my body in that possessive air, he wants me.

"Because deep down you're a good guy and you know that a person is not a poker chip."

"That's where you're wrong," he says, "that's exactly what a person is. You, me, we're all just poker chips moved around by the whims of the circus gods."

I roll my eyes. Circus people are a superstitious bunch of people, so I wouldn't be surprised to hear this from most, but I don't believe the words that are coming out of his mouth right now. This is a man who used a very practical, non-mystical way of getting what he wanted.

"You can collect money from him," I say, "but you're not collecting me."

"You're worth so much more than money."

The words should not make me blush, but they do.

I've been under my father's thumb for way too long knowing that I'm only worth the next night's ticket sales to him.

"The games don't count for anything," I say. "The games in that trailer, most of the time they're cheating."

"Which makes it that much more humiliating that they lost," he says.

He's not wrong about that, but I'm not about to agree with him on anything. "Look, all my friends are here. My family is here."

His expression softens just a bit. "You'll make new friends, new family. One that won't expect you to do tricks like that triple flip, which was too dangerous and the crowd barely even understood what they were seeing, how much technique it took."

A shiver runs through me because it means that he did see me.

He did know how much technique it took.

The risk, well, there's always a risk of falling. You don't become a trapeze artist because you're afraid of the ground. You become a trapeze artist because you love to fly. And nothing, absolutely nothing feels as good as landing that triple flip.

"I like that trick," I say mildly, my voice not betraying any of the hours and hours of practice, any of the pain of falling again and again and again, or the hurt of my father turning away from me, not bothering to spare me a glance until I nailed it every time.

That was a while ago.

I wouldn't do it for him now. Now I perform for someone else.

"I like that trick," I tell him, "I'm going to keep doing it. In fact, nothing feels as good as doing that trick and landing it, nothing."

The corner of his lips quirk up. "Nothing feels as good? That's interesting because I can think of at least one thing that should feel better."

Sex. He's talking about sex.

I force myself to frown at him even though there's a tug of curiosity in my gut, a whisper that wonders if it really could feel better. Not with anyone, not with any man, but with this man specifically. He said he could make me like it and something about his confidence, something about the casual air of insouciance he carries around.

It fits as well as his bespoke jacket.

It also makes me think he might be right. "Your male pride probably couldn't handle anyone telling you something else," I say, my voice tart.

He gives me a lazy smile. "I know when a woman is faking it, sweetheart, and if you spent the night with me, you would not have to fake a single moan, a single whimper, a single orgasm as I made you come over and over again."

There's heat between my legs, surprising considering how cold it is outside and considering the situation, which is that he thinks he won me in a freaking poker game. Not going to happen, out of the question except every second that I spend with him, it feels a little more plausible. It feels a little bit more like the deal has already been done and I'm just arguing against the inevitable.

"I've been with Blue Moon my whole life," I whisper, "I can't just leave."

"We have better working hours, actual healthcare benefits. We'll set you up for a comfortable life, retirement."

I scoff, "Retirement? I'm lucky if I can think a few days ahead."

"Well, you should be," he says, "Performers can't work beyond a certain age, at least not doing the same kind of shows. The circus likes to churn people up and then spit them back out, but not ours. Logan Whitmere treats his staff with respect."

I give him a suspicious look, "And does he know that you're here recruiting talent with a poker game?"

A flicker in his dark eyes tells me the answer is, no. "It doesn't matter how I get you there. All you need to know is that once you're there, you'll be treated like acrobatic royalty. You'll get your own show. You'll headline something that actually makes national news. You'll become renowned. Everyone will know your act and come see you."

I snort. "I don't do this for the accolades."

"Unlikely," he says, "every performer does it for the accolades."

"Well, I don't."

"Then what do you do it for?"

I started it out of fear and I suppose despite everything that's happened in all the years and all the strength I've built and the defenses I've erected, that's still the reason why I do it. A sad commentary that I have no plan on sharing with this stranger. "It doesn't matter why I perform when you want me for more than that."

"So your true objection has to do with jumping into my bed?"

"I'm not jumping in anywhere," I say, "not your circus and definitely not your bed."

"Has someone been clumsy with you, ma chère?" he says, the French lilt running over my arms like the softest fur, leaving a bristle of pleasure. "Has some old-fashioned acrobat lured you into his bed only to rut on you and leave you wanting? How remiss of him."

I don't want to think about sex, at least not actual sex that I've had in the past.

In fact, if you would've asked me a few minutes ago, I would've said I never like to think about sex ever. All of that seems to have changed now that I've met Emerson Durand. He's the absolute embodiment of sex. He walks like it, talks like it, smells like it, looks like it. No wonder he assumes I'm just going to fall into his bed because he won some stupid game. Women probably throw themselves at him for no reason at all.

"You would be disappointed," I tell him, my voice icy, the same voice that makes my father's friends laugh and call me the ice queen. Not that I care, let them talk, at least they stay away from me for the most part.

None of them can afford to pay my father enough for the privilege.

"Well," he says, "we're going to find out, aren't we?"

I take a step back. "We're not."

He gives me a hard smile. "You don't want to test me on this. I won you, which means you're mine."

"I don't agree to this."

"You may tell that to Logan Whitmere when you see him. Perhaps, he'll care more about your wishes."

I back up, thinking about running.

That's when a black SUV pulls up behind me. I jump because there were no headlights and barely any sound. I didn't know it was coming. Another man jumps out and then I'm hustled toward the car. His two friends must have known this was happening because they exit my father's trailer and then there are bodies moving me.

It's hard to explain because none of them actually hurt me.

None of them manhandle me the way that I'm used to, but somehow their bodies move me in a flow until I'm practically inside the car.

I catch myself at the door half inside, the warmth of the interior, the smooth leather, the safeness of it calls to me. It's a siren call, a fake call because there's not really safety inside there.

Emerson frowns. "You aren't going to give me trouble, are you?"

"Tell me one reason why I should go with you, one real reason, and don't tell me about the game. Don't tell me about the health benefits. Tell me something about you."

"Me?" He looks up at the sky, at the millions of stars that are only visible when we're far away from the city. When he looks back at me, at least one portion of the mask has dropped.

I'm seeing the real him, the real man beneath the ringmaster's mask.

"I'm a man who cannot be trusted," he says, "even by his closest friends. I'm a liar, a cheat. I hurt people I care about, and the ones I don't care about, I hurt even worse."

"None of this is making me trust you," I whisper.

"Trust me? No, you don't need to trust me. You would be a fool to trust me. All you have to know is that I recorded our entire game and if you stay here, I will broadcast it. Your father will be a mockery. He'll be outcast. Is that what you want for him?"

I pause, my breath in my throat. If that happened, if my father was humiliated in that way he would take it out on me. Even worse, he would take it out on Seraphina. Except how can I leave her here?

Emerson clearly expects me to drop everything behind, even my clothes and toiletries.

He expects me to leave right now and he has a reason.

My father is probably inside his trailer plotting how to hurt him.

In fact, it's inevitable. Whether I go or stay, my father will come for me.

I need to think fast and smart if I'm going to keep me safe and Sera safe throughout this. I bite my lip. The longer we stay here, the more likely my father is to come out with a rifle and then all hell will break loose.

There will be shooting, potentially worse, and Seraphina will be right in the middle of it. No, I need to draw this away from her or get her away somehow. For a brief moment, I consider trusting Emerson with the truth and seeing what he would do, but he's already told me I would be a fool to trust him. And Seraphina isn't legally mine, so however much his circus may want me to headline their new show, they're not going to be a party to kidnapping.

My eyes fall closed in temporary despair.

I need to go now, but I can fix this. I am coming up with a plan.

Reluctantly I get into the SUV.

An inscrutable look crosses Emerson's handsome face.

"It won't be so bad. You aren't going to the guillotine, mademoiselle."

He barely has time to get the word out before my father's trailer slams open. Emerson jumps inside after me and then we're zooming away leaving the fairgrounds behind us, my heart in my throat.

Chapter Four

Emerson

We are staying at the nicest hotel in Boise, which isn't saying much.

There are white sheets and mediocre room service, so five stars, I suppose.

We're also staying in the presidential suite, which has two bedrooms ostensibly so we can have two different people sleep in separate beds. That won't be happening tonight, but the illusion calmed Luna down. When she entered, she retreated into her bedroom and I allowed her to do so because I needed to secure our location. Alex is one of the guys I trust the most. He has a blind devotion to me, which really is the level of devotion that I require.

"It is clear, boss," he says.

I watch the street where cars roll past in the cool early spring air. Nothing is happening, but Rider will have to make his move tonight. He knows I'm going to get her out of the state tomorrow. As soon as we can get on a flight. Then we will be in Nebraska. "Should we call Whitmere?" he asks.

"Not yet," I say. I'm not sure exactly how I want to present her, but I have time, a few hours at least, and most likely a fight before that.

"You have the exits covered?" I ask.

He nods. "Jeremy and Rocky are stationed downstairs. We've also got a car ready to go. If anything happens, we can bolt."

"We're not bolting," I say, "this is our turf. Rider and his men don't belong here."

Alex nods. "Yes, sir."

He doesn't question me out loud, but I can tell he's wondering, why aren't we calling Whitmere? Why don't we get their help? I've got a few strong men with me, but I could get more. It's not quite that simple. Don't tell anyone I reiterate, even though I've already given this instruction. No calls, no texts, nothing. Circuses aren't exactly known for keeping secrets very well, especially within their own ranks, but I need Alex to keep his mouth shut when it comes to the rest of Cirque des Miroirs.

"Dinner?" he asks.

"Have something sent up," I answer. "Something substantial. Steaks, whatever they have that the chef recommends." He nods and heads into the hallway. He has a room next door for easy access and security purposes. I stare out the window a little longer until the lights become red x's through the glass. I may have told a teeny tiny lie to Rider about the offer from Logan Whitmere. It didn't exactly come from him.

Everyone in the industry knows about Luna Rider, about her talent.

She would've been poached years ago if she were willing to leave, but we all also know about her father and no one is willing to do what it takes to separate her.

No one's willing to do what it takes except me.

That's what I did tonight.

I had the balls to do it.

I had the courage, which means I get all the glory and all the rewards. Like Luna Rider in my bed. Do I feel guilty about that? No. I feel proud, and when I bring her back to Logan, he will be forced to concede that I'm exactly what the circus needs.

He will rescind my little firing, my little banishment.

All of that will be forgotten.

All of it will be forgiven, once I bring such premier talent.

I knock on her door.

There's a long pause. She expected me to leave her alone tonight. Unlikely.

"Come in." She's barely said the words before I'm opening the door as if she might be able to climb through windows that don't open and somehow rappel down five stories. I'm not taking any chances. I lean against the doorframe, studying her where she sits up on the bed. She hasn't gone under the covers. She's still wearing a tracksuit from earlier. I bet there's a leotard underneath the jacket. The blue one, the leotard with sparkles.

Luna Rider should have been safely tucked away in bed at the time of the already infamous poker game. Even if someone had heard the ruckus and woken her up, she would've been changed into pajamas or something else. Instead, it's like she never went to bed.

"You run the place, don't you?" I ask, my voice low.

Her brow furrows. "Run what place?"

"Blue Moon. The whole thing. You do it. You run the whole thing for your father. It's not just the show. It's everything else."

She looks away, her cheeks flushed. Guilty.

What must it be like to have the devotion of this woman, the loyalty of this woman that she would run an entire circus, that she would reject offer after offer for more safety, more security, more money, more fame in order to maintain your rundown circus?

I'll never know because I'll never have a daughter.

And that's the only way men like me would ever know that kind of love.

Men like Michael Rider, because yes, he and I are the same.

"You don't owe him. Look at all the years you've done this for him. And he throws you away on a gamble. You don't need to feel guilty for leaving."

Her voice is thicker. "You don't know anything about anything."

"Then tell me," I say, stepping deeper into the room. There's plush carpet and fancy art on the walls, but none of it's real. None of it's genuine. None of it's true quality except for the woman who's sitting there looking lost and a little afraid. She's holding both arms around herself, hugging herself for comfort.

That's what I want to do, hug her, touch her, comfort her, but I know that my touch wouldn't actually be comforting to her right now. She shakes her head refusing to confide in me, which is fair, but inconvenient.

"I just want to sleep," she says, which is her way of saying she wants me to leave.

"Not likely. Neither of us will be getting much sleep tonight."

Her gray gaze snaps to mine at the innuendo, which yes, is exactly what I meant. For a moment, I give her relief. I give her peace, which is confusing all on its own.

"Your father's going to make a try for you. He doesn't intend for me to live to see tomorrow."

Her eyes widen in shock. Not at the accusation, but at the realization that I know this.

A soft laugh escapes me. "Yes, your father's reputation precedes him. Though I don't need rumors to understand him, I already know everything he would do."

"And how's that?" she asks, looking doubtful.

"He and I are both reptilian, cold, lethal. And that's what I would do if someone tried to take you from me. Whatever it took to get you back."

Even a few feet away, I can see the shiver that overtakes her. "I don't belong to anybody."

I smile and reach into my pocket. One of the cheap cracked poker chips is inside there. I pull it out and toss it to her. It spins in the air, red and white stripes. She catches it between her palms then looks at it.

"We're all chips," I tell her. "Moving around on the table. It's only an illusion that we're ever the hand that moves them."

"So what?" she asks, standing, her chin rising in defiance. "I should just sleep with you because there's no other choice, because we're all just chips, because decisions are just an illusion?"

"Everything is an illusion." I back her up against the wall close enough that I can scent her unique feminine flavor, that I can almost, almost taste it just from smell alone.

The urge to bury my face in the crook of her neck is strong, but I fight it.

I fight it so I can tell her choice is an illusion.

Dreams are an illusion, so why shouldn't reality be the same way?

Why are dreams the sole providence of hope and pleasure and peace?

Why can't we have it right now?

And then I can't help myself. I bring my hand up to her face and cup her gently as if her body is made for mine. Her face tilts up and our mouths are inches away, and then closer, closer until I can feel her warm rapid breath against my lips like a caress.

"If it's all an illusion," I whisper, "then let's make it one to enjoy."

I kiss her like I've kissed a thousand women, women before her. It should be the same. It should mean nothing. It should be pleasurable long enough to draw me out of my head so I stop thinking, thinking, thinking. That's why I'm charming after all.

That's why I fuck beautiful women in every town, so that I can enter my body and escape my mind even if it's fleeting, even if it's only minutes at a time. But something about this lets me sit in my mind and my body. Something about this keeps me fully aware. Even as I lose myself inside her, my body is on fire. Yes, I feel pleasure. I feel desire. I feel an overwhelming urge to bury my cock inside her. All of those things are true, and yet I'm also fully aware, fully alive.

Desire swirls in the air around us.

Shadows mixed with light, making this moment more real than any I've had before. Her flavor imprints on me. It's more than a memory and many years from now when she's long gone, living some beautiful life, probably having forgotten me, and I'm ruined, ruined, ruined.

I'll know this scent.

When I wake up, it will be the last thing I remember tasting, before I fall asleep.

I devour her wanting more, more, more. I lick into her mouth, drawing away the flavor as if I can own it, as if I can consume every part of her, every drop she moans into my mouth.

There's surprise in her reaction. She wasn't expecting a kiss. Yes, yes, I understand that much. We weren't supposed to be kissing, at least not if I want her to feel safe, not if I really want to take her to Logan. I shouldn't be doing this, but I can't stop, I can't fucking stop.

There's more than surprise though.

There's innocence as if she hasn't kissed much in her life and she isn't sure what to do. I'm not usually with an inexperienced woman. I like big, bold, sexy women who know what they want, who aren't afraid to ask for it, demand it. But her naïveté mixed with that gentle questioning nudge of her tongue is almost enough to unman me.

It's as if she wants to please me.

She just doesn't know how.

And that combination sets fire to something primal inside me.

My cock throbs in my slacks, my hands shake with the effort to be gentle. One still cupped around her jaw, the other pulling her hips close to me so she can feel me. "This is what you do to me," I mutter to her. "This is how crazy you make me."

"It's how crazy you make every man and many of the women in the audience each night. Do you know that? Does it bother you? Do you mind or is it irrelevant to you as you soar so high above everyone?" A low whimper is my only answer. She's beyond thought. Her hard nipples showing through the thin material of her jacket. She leans back languidly against the hotel wall.

"What are you doing to me?" she asks, her voice hoarse.

I drop my mouth to her ear and say, almost soundless, "I'm freeing you, freeing her." What a lie. What a joke. What a little deception I'm playing except that in the end, when I'm long gone, this young woman will be free. I'll make sure of it. I only have to hold on to her for a little bit. I only have to suck a little of her vitality into my body to hold on to it, to hoard it like a dragon with its treasure, sleeping on it in his cave. That's what I'll be like using the knowledge of her body to keep me warm on long and endless nights. "I've never done this before," she whispers.

"Done what… sex in the presidential suite of a five-star hotel?" No, probably not. Maybe she's never been with someone like me. Someone experienced. Something about the image of her with some fumbling young acrobat, both of them tumbling around like cubs, comforts me. Not because I want anyone to have touched her. There is a very possessive masculine part of me that doesn't want that, but I like the picture. It presents the sweetness that she got the care he must have taken even if he ended up fumbling, even if she ended up unsatisfied.

That won't happen this time. Not with me. There won't be any laughter when we have sex. There won't be much experimentation or discovery, at least not for me. I've done everything before and I'm going to walk her through it piece by piece, position by position, taste by taste for as long as I have with her. However short, I will show her what to do.

Her heavy-lidded gaze studies me. "Maybe we can have this night," she says as if it's only just occurred to her that we might actually do it, that we might actually have sex tonight. When really it was a foregone conclusion, it was always a certainty. After I saw her up close in that leotard, her lithe body ready for me.

Maybe I can have one night, one night already. She's planning an end after one night. I agree easily because I'm a liar and the deception doesn't bother me even a little bit. I tug down the zipper of her jacket and push the wispy fabric aside. It's far too thin for her to be outside in this weather, especially considering there's only a leotard underneath, the same leotard she was wearing earlier today. I slide a hand underneath it right above her collarbone and then push the strap off her shoulder, one then the other. I tug them lower and lower until her small tight breasts appear. She's trapped, all tied up, the fabric pressing into her muscular arms.

Her nipples taut with desire.

Does she even know what she wants from me?

I lean down to suck one and she cries out in surprise. Her hands go to my hair. It's more than just support they need. As they clutch the long strands, she's combing through it, brushing it with her fingers, letting it glide over her palms, glorying in it.

Yes, I'm a vain man. I know how good my face looks, all angular and sharp.

I know what my hair does to women.

Hell, women and men alike love my lean, cut body.

It's always brought me pleasure knowing that, knowing the effect I have on people, the arousal I create in them. I've used it to my advantage plenty of times, but it's never felt quite like this. Those other times it was just a coincidence, a matter of happenstance that I existed in this form and that someone else found it attractive.

Now with this woman, it feels necessary. Like I need to be what she wants or I would expire on the spot. The way she strokes my hair, feeling it, wanting it, makes me so hot.

She might as well be sucking on my cock.

I grunt my pleasure, letting her know what she does to me. I pull the leotard lower and lower still until she steps out of it. She moves slowly, almost lethargic as if she's in a daze, revealing herself to me. She's shaved bare everywhere, most likely so it doesn't affect the lines of her costume. It doesn't matter why she did it, though. The effect is the same—startling, breathtaking. It's an electric current through my body and so I don't bother to stand. It wouldn't feel right looming over her, a solid foot taller than her and heavier, too.

That isn't what I want to do right now.

Maybe another time I'll hold her down. I'll tie her up.

There are a million ways I want to have her, but for right now, I want her this way, her slender legs spread before me, kneeling between them. Her naked, me fully clothed, my mouth fucking her clit, licking and licking, drinking her down until her cries bounce off the molded ceilings.

She fights it until the very end, holding back. Her thighs trembling almost as if she doesn't want to come. It's only in the final moments when she tugs my hair hard enough that tears prick my eyes, it's when she lets out an uneven moan that I realize she doesn't know what's coming.

She doesn't know.

It hits her without warning.

This first time, the *only* time she's ever come.

Chapter Five

Luna

I'm shaking, shivering, leaning against the wall.

I would slide down except for Emerson's hands on me holding me up.

He looks at me with pure shock. He wants an explanation, but I can't give him one. I have done brutal training sessions. I've been injured during them. Major injuries that I had to nurse back to health in my trailer with limited supplies.

I've been beaten by my father and worse.

Through all of it, I was able to be stoic, almost calm.

Well, it probably wasn't a healthy calm, a form of detachment, dissociation.

No one knew I was upset even if they saw my father backhand me.

Keeping my cool is what allowed me to survive.

"All these years you've never come before," he said, and then as a thought just occurred to him, "Are you a virgin?"

"No," I say, shoving him away, but my hands have no power behind them.

They're like spaghetti noodles.

His eyes narrow. "Did I hurt you?"

Did he hurt me? It's a complicated question.

No, there was no physical pain, but somehow it opened a dam inside me, a dam full of emotional pain. Who knew that pleasure could be the key that unlocked it, that would open Pandora's box? That it would let out all of my demons?

They invade my body, making me tremble.

"I've done this before," I say, my teeth chattering.

I've made myself come before, a pillow between my legs, riding it quietly until there's a small spark of relief. It was nothing like this, nothing like the detonation of desire that just happened in my body. It turned me inside out, his mouth on my sex, his hair in my hands.

It wasn't only pleasure. It was control.

No, I didn't control him. That would be foolish to believe.

Not for a second did I have any control in this situation, but it was something else.

Consent maybe.

Or maybe it has nothing to do with me and it's just this man. Maybe he's able to turn all women inside out through his pure undiluted handsomeness. Then again, if that were true, he wouldn't look concerned right now.

"Chère," he says, using a French endearment. "What's wrong?"

Drawing from a strength deep inside me, I force myself to stand up. Work, I tell my limbs, you have to work. This is a performance, as surely as the ones I give under the big top.

I give him a strained smile. "It just took me by surprise," I say. "A few hours ago, I had never even met you. And now, here we are naked in a hotel room."

I glance down at his clothes. The lines of his suit are beautiful.

Everything about him is beautiful.

Even the bulge that demonstrates his arousal. It should be vulgar, crass. Instead, even that looks elegant on this man. He doesn't look convinced, but now that I'm not about to topple over, he does release me and step back.

"I moved too fast," he says, though it's not meant for me. He's muttering to himself.

He moved too fast. Yes, that's true enough, but moving at any speed would've been a shock to my system. I've never experienced anything like this.

There's a knock, a distant knock.

He glances up, distracted. "That will be dinner." My gaze slides sideways to the bed, which is still fully made, only the slightest indent, showing where my body lay on top of it. It's about where he and I could lay, where he could do that to me again, where he could show me what else I never knew.

A small part of me longs for that, but most of me is terrified. "Great," I say. "I am super hungry."

My movements are jerky as I pull my clothes on, covering myself.

Emerson is clearly skeptical, but he allows me to walk past him and leave the hotel room into the shared area of the suite. Actually, I've never even been in a hotel room like this. Occasionally, rarely, we've stopped and for some reason needed a motel instead of the RVs. I've seen what they look like, dingy smelling of smoke, bathrooms full of mold. They have nothing to do with this place.

First of all, there are multiple rooms in one, multiple doors that I don't even know where they lead. Two bedrooms. It looks like each with their own large bathroom suite, an area with a dining table, a set of couches and large TV, another half bath, a bar area, and a view that overlooks a dusky skyline.

One of the men Emerson had with him is setting up a cart that has a built-in little table with flaps that come up, a white tablecloth and a couple dishes covered with metal domes.

He gives me a brief, polite, impersonal nod before disappearing out the door again.

I wander over and lift the domes. One side is a steak. I'll leave that for Emerson. The other plate has fish covered with an herb sauce. There's a side of bright vegetables, broccoli, carrots, zucchini. I sit down on that side and begin eating because I am actually ravenous. I haven't eaten since breakfast, which now feels like an entire lifetime ago.

Emerson seats himself, his dark eyes hooded.

It looks like he wants to ask more, probe more, but I pray that he doesn't.

I'm not sure how strong my defenses are right now.

They feel like they're made of wet paper.

"What happened at the Olympics?" he asks, taking a bite of steak.

Of course, he chooses that moment to attack, and of course he chooses that moment to attack in a way that I didn't expect. I thought he would tell me more about this magical deal that I'm being offered at his circus.

Instead, he asks me about the past, about that dark period I'm forced to remember. Any other time I could have given him a flippant answer or ignored him. I have a lot of experience fielding that question since people always want to know. One minute I'm on a high, having won nationals, a star Olympic hopeful, getting calls from Nike and Peloton about endorsement deals.

The next minute, it crashed.

There was a brief blip where everyone, in the world it seemed like, was wondering what happened. An Olympic hopeful, especially one who had been predicted to do so well for the U.S. gymnastics team doesn't just vanish. She doesn't just *not show up*.

That's exactly what I did.

"I wouldn't know," I manage, my voice icy. "I never set foot inside the Olympic Village."

He studies me. "Nerves?"

His voice is polite, a little impersonal. I laugh. "I guess you could say that."

He cuts into his steak and takes a bite. Taking his time. "Perhaps you decided you didn't want to represent this country. After all, performing for the circus has no such political implications."

I take a bite of fish, not answering that political affiliations had nothing to do with the reason why I didn't go to the Olympics. I would've loved to hold up the American flag at the opening ceremony. I would've loved to be a part of a team of other women like me who only cared about flying. It was a dream too big for me to even have until I was scouted. The money, the fame, none of that mattered to me, but it mattered to my father.

He agreed because he thought he could come along for the ride like one of those pageant moms, except he was a dad and I was already twelve. My act at the circus wasn't drawing that much attention at the time. So the fact that I had to be training for most of the year didn't bother him. I was in heaven… and the Blue Moon Circus? Well, the circus was floundering. It was struggling. The money I was bringing in through endorsement deals helped with that. Of course, it went to him and not me, but I didn't care. All of my equipment was provided for me through those deals. I worked with a coach also provided by the U.S. gymnastics team. I lived in a dorm with the other hopefuls. School was something I could knock out in a few hours a week with a tutor. "It was the happiest time of my life," I say.

"I'm sure," he says, knowing, a little smug about it, which makes me want to reach over the table and punch him in the face. Even though I've never had a violent thought in my life.

All the times when my father hit me, I never once thought about hitting back.

It's only this man, Emerson Durand, who can induce violence out of me.

"Then it was your father who stopped you," he says, sounding almost bored. "The most predictable answer, but then that's the way of the world, isn't it? Ockham's razor, the simplest answer is the correct one."

"Yes," I say, bitterness souring my tone. "I guess you could say it was my father."

"He decided he didn't like his little girl being so far away from him. Is that it? Or he figured he could make more money out of you if you had to come back and perform for the circus." He takes another bite, chewing thoughtfully. "A little shortsighted of him, of course. You do get press, local small press along with the questions. What happened? Where was she? Why didn't she show up? The mystery might add to it, but, overall, it's small time, right? That's what his circus has always been. Small time."

I glare at him. "This is none of your business."

"Everything about you is my business. Remember, I own you now."

I look away and my jaw clenches. He owns me and he held me against a wall and licked my clit until I came so hard I saw stars. He told me earlier that there was one thing that felt better than flying. I understand now what he meant about the intensity of it, but I can't say that it felt *good*. That word doesn't seem to apply to something that felt more like the big bang at the start of the universe, like an implosion, like my atoms came together and then broke apart, forming something new.

"Then again," he says, continuing despite my non-answer, "your father is a shortsighted man. After all, he gambled you, didn't he?

Thinking he could make some quick money off of me."

"More likely he didn't care about the outcome of the game and he was planning on killing you. Did you ever think of that? That you weren't safe? That you still aren't safe?"

He gives me a long slow smile. "Worried about me, ma chère? How darling. How sweet."

"Of course you thought about it," I say. "You brought friends, armed friends."

"Friends," he says, tasting the word as if for the first time. "Those men are loyal to me, but they don't know me. And beyond what I need to know to make them useful, I don't know them. I'm not a man who has friends."

I've eaten about half what's on the plate and part of me knows that my body needs more nutrition in order to make it through this night and the coming day.

But I can't stomach another bite. I shove the plate away and stand up. "You want to know what happened all those years ago? I'll tell you."

I've never told anyone else, but I look around. The laugh that comes out of me is slightly manic. Nothing else seems to be happening according to plan, and the truth is, I'm not going to see this man after today. Either way, whether my father succeeds in hurting him or whether he doesn't, we're going to be done. I'm going to escape. Go back to the Blue Moon.

It's what has to happen, so I might as well tell him the truth.

It doesn't matter if he knows.

"I got blackmailed," I say. "Or more specifically, my father got blackmailed since he was the one in charge of the money I was getting for endorsements."

Eyes narrow, those dark eyes glitter. "Blackmailed for what? I'm sure there's no shortage of things your father has done."

A short, harsh laugh, erupts. No, it's not a laugh. It's a sob. "They could have blackmailed him for any number of things that wouldn't have ruined my chances. No, it was blackmail for things I did."

"You were a young girl. What could you have done?"

I gesture wildly toward the bedroom where I had been resting, toward the bedroom where he tore me apart. "You asked me in there if

I was a virgin. How silly," I say, trying to achieve a mocking tone like his. "How silly that you would think that when I've had sex plenty of times, early and often."

Realization sweeps over his features after all, my father all but confessed in his trailer, didn't he? That's what narcissists do. They blame you for things that they themselves have done. He said that Emerson and his circus would sell me to the highest bidder, would allow their VIP ticket holders to have sex with me for the right price, which means that's what he did to me.

I see the awareness rock through Emerson's eyes, disbelief, horror, fury.

Distantly, very distantly, I know that I should be gratified by his reaction. That he doesn't just smile and say that I probably deserved it or that I probably enjoyed it distantly. I recognize that there's still humanity left inside him despite all of his claims to the contrary, but I'm far away from that feeling now, I'm detached. I have found my dissociation again and there's so much blessed relief inside of it because I'm tired of feeling things.

This man makes me feel too much.

"Yes," I tell him. "That's right. He sold me to whoever was willing to pay enough. One of those men, when they saw me on the news as an Olympic hopeful, decided to get some of that endorsement money and if my father had just paid it, if my father had just fucking paid, I could have gone to the Olympics. I could have had an entirely different life. But he didn't."

"I'm going to kill him," Emerson says almost conversationally.

I don't know whether he's talking about my father or the faceless man who decided to come back and blackmail us. I never even knew which one of them it was. I'm not sure I would even recognize him if I saw a photo of him. I tried not to look at them. I tried not to remember them, but I remember each night. I remember each city that it happened, the unique scents and sounds of the place, the fauna. I remember the places where I was defiled by more than the men who did it. My father thought the man was bluffing, that he wouldn't actually do anything, but it turns out it was worse than that.

"The man told my coach. He told the U.S. gymnastics team." They pulled me aside, asked if it was true. I didn't know what to say. I was afraid, so I told the truth. "I was told the night before I was supposed to get on a plane not to show up, that I wouldn't be welcome and that if I just left quietly, there would be no inquiry, no public statements. They would just wonder. The public would wonder forever and that would be preferable to the team having to kick me off publicly using their morality clause."

Emerson stands up practically vibrating with rage. His dark eyes flashing like a night sky in a storm. "How dare they?" he says, on a growl. "How fucking dare they?"

I laugh, but it's hollow. I've had a long time to grow accustomed to these facts and yet they never seem to fit. Like square blocks in circular holes. I can't ever just put them away. I can't ever be done with them. They follow me around day after day when little girls come up to me after a show and ask me to autograph for them. When they tell me they dream about being a gymnast, about being in the Olympics, I have to smile and tell them I believe in them. You can do it, and the weirdest part is that it's not a lie. I do believe in them.

It's only me.

Only me who never really belonged there, only me who was asked to leave.

"Some days I think it would've been better," I say, "to let it all come out, to let them expel me from the team for the morality clause. The shame would've been almost unbearable, but somehow, somehow the mystery of it, the questions, they're worse."

Chapter Six

Emerson

Every cell in my body wants to go after her, to hold her down, to make her tell me every detail, to snarl and fight and kill everyone who ever touched her, to fuck her until she forgets every single one of those times. To hold her.

I think that's the most alarming impulse—holding her.

I've had sex with a lot of women in my past, but I've never wanted, never longed to hold them, and that's it. I fight the impulse because for maybe the first time in my life, I'm out of my depth.

It seemed so easy to saunter into her circus. To find a way to take her, to keep her, to own her, to fuck her, because that's what I did, isn't it? I laid down money on her father's poker table. I can still taste her orgasm on my tongue.

Maybe that's why I let her retreat into her room.

Maybe that's why I feel like shit. Because I'm not much better than those men that used her, than the ones who crushed her dreams. That's the reason I sit in an armchair, staring at her door, brooding. There's a glass of scotch next to me, but I don't have it in me to drink.

I don't want to numb the pain.

I just want to feel it because that's what she had to do, isn't it?

The worst part is knowing that I would do it all over again.

Even as I curse every man who used her for his own dark purposes, including myself. I savor the taste of her on my tongue. It makes me hard just thinking about it.

Vlad comes and goes, I sent him away so she can rest.

Maybe she's getting a few minutes of sleep, or maybe she's in there plotting her escape.

Either way, I need to get us out of this state and fast, even if I feel guilty for what I did to her. Her confession only strengthens my resolve to get her away from her father for good.

This time, as dawn breaks, I open the door only to discover the room is empty, the bathroom door's open a crack, the light off. I know before I even push the door open and peek into the empty shower and tub that she's gone.

I can feel it.

Her absence, it's like a living, breathing thing, eating me up inside.

We're hundreds of feet in the air. No way she went out the window, but her exit becomes clear. There's one of those connecting doors, the kind you have to unlock on both sides in order to open.

And it's unlocked.

I swing the door open to reveal another hotel room smaller than this. On the other side, it's a mirror to the one that Vlad is staying in across from the suite. Shock runs threw me, along with frustration and reluctant amusement.

At least some part of her enjoyed escaping my clutches.

Then again, she would've gone right back to her father.

Now, that I can't stand for.

Is he going to punish her for what happened, for making him look like a fool, even though I'm the one who did it? Probably. Small men like that. Scared men punish the women in their lives, and he has a long history of it with her.

I glance at my watch. Six a.m. There's not much time.

It doesn't take long to gather Vlad and the other guys. We have two black SUVs that we ride along the country roads to where the circus used to be, praying they haven't already packed up. And God bless their inefficiency. Honestly, God bless the fact that her father could not run this place without her because everything is still askew, half put together, half taken apart.

When we pull up, tires screeching, men and women watch our

arrival. But they don't try to stop us, which says something about the person who runs the circus.

There's no loyalty here.

He hasn't earned any.

We arrive at his RV, which looks even sadder and more dingy in the daylight. It's old, which is disturbing because it means he's probably had it for a long time, which means that this is where Luna used to live. This is where she lived until the Olympic Committee plucked her out of obscurity. They would have whisked her away somewhere that might have seemed too strict and too sparse for someone else but to her it must have felt like winning the lottery.

It must have been incredibly luxurious to live from breath to breath without fear, without filth. I don't bother knocking, but kick the door in, my YSL shoes doing the job.

My two old friends back at the Cirque des Miroirs, Logan and Wolfgang, stomp around with their big heavy work boots to show they mean business. Me? I dress with style, with flair, and I mean business at the same time.

I expect to find Luna inside.

I'm not disappointed.

I also expect to find her father here.

What I don't expect is a little girl.

She doesn't have their coloring, not the blonde hair, not the gray eyes. Instead, she has black hair, black eyes, and tan skin. There's a little girl somehow caught in the middle of this, a little girl that I didn't know about.

She looks terrified, tears streaming down her face.

My gut clenches. A child. Who the fuck is this child? I throw up my hand to stop Vlad and the other guys who are already armed with their guns out blazing. I don't want them to shoot. Not when there's a child involved.

"Did you forget your toothbrush?" I ask Luna in a calm voice. I need to de-escalate the situation, which is not something I'm used to doing. Everything I do, everything I am as a ringmaster is about making things bigger, more dramatic, more intense.

That can't happen here.

Not if we all want to walk away from this safely.

Her dad has clearly been drinking in the time that we have been gone. His eyes are bloodshot. Well, one of his eyes, the other one is swollen shut from when I punched him for talking shit about his own daughter.

His hold is too hard on the little girl. I can see the way her tan skin turns pale where his fingers grip her. I'm going to give him another black eye to match the one he already has.

First, I need to get him away from everyone else.

"You should go," Luna says, her voice calm and steady. "You don't belong here."

Neither do you. That's what I want to tell her, but I don't because it would only piss off her father. "Listen, I tell him. This is between you and me. Let's have a conversation, man to man. We can let the girls go sleep it off. Let them go."

He snarls at me. "This is all your fault. This happened because you came here."

My stomach tenses because he's right. I've always done whatever I wanted to do whenever I wanted to do it without regard for the consequences, and now there are two consequences. Luna and this little girl who I don't even know her name.

"You took her from me," he says, snarling, his eyes wild.

"I could never take her from you," I tell him, reaching down to the dregs of my humanity for some old-fashioned honesty. Even with crazy eyes, even drunk and enraged, people can tell when you're being honest. That's what I do right now. I tell him the truth. "I could never take her from you because I'm just like you. I am someone who grasps at whatever I can, tries to take whatever I can to steal, cheat."

His eyes widen. "You cheated."

"That's right. I cheated. I cheated in that card game, which means I didn't really win her."

The fact that they were cheating too doesn't matter.

The only thing that matters right now is calming everyone down and getting that little girl away from him. "Why don't we let the girls go outside, do whatever girls do. We can settle this like men, okay? You and me. You and me, we're going to figure this out together. We're going to shake hands at the end of this, right?"

A little doubt enters his mind, a little uncertainty, a little distrust. "You're trying to screw me. This is another trick."

"If it was a trick, I'd say I could already grab her and be gone, right? I don't need that little girl for my show. She's not part of the act that I need. She doesn't have an offer with the circus. She's just some random kid, and you and I both know we don't care about random kids. That's how we operate. They're collateral. The fact that I'm standing here, that's because I want to make a deal with you because I want to make this work out for everyone. The circuses have to stick together, right?"

This is where I'm going off script a little bit. This is no longer the truth. Circuses don't really stick together. In fact, they're pretty cutthroat. We're competition, but I'm hoping he doesn't think too hard about that right now. He's too busy thinking about all the money he might make if Luna actually comes back to the show.

"Everything can be like it was," I say. "You can have the great Luna Rider flying in your show, and I'll go back where I came from."

He narrows his eyes. "You'll go back where you came from and what? Delete that recording of the game. The game where you cheated."

"Already done. It's gone. No one will ever know what happened that night. No one needs to know what happened tonight. This is private business, right? We don't let the town see private business. That, at least, you understand."

He nods. "Yeah. Yeah. It's private business."

"Exactly," I say, "so let the little girl go to sleep or school or wherever the fuck she's supposed to be. She doesn't need to be part of this. Looks like you guys are packing up outside, so you and I will just talk while they close up all the equipment, right? That's all."

Slowly, slowly, he releases her, and then with a pained cry, she flies into Luna's arms.

Luna holds her tight.

Despite the differences in their appearance, it's clear they have a close bond.

Mother and daughter?

The idea makes me feel stricken. Did one of the assholes her father sold her to knock her up? It makes my blood boil, and now that the little girl's out of the way, there's nothing holding me back. I slam my fist into Michael Rider's jaw. He crumples. Shit, I did it too hard. Not that I mind hurting him, but I wanted to drag it out, torture him like he deserves. I turn around to find Luna facing me, her chin raised, her gray eyes full of fire, silver fire. "You want me to do your show?" she asks.

I narrow my eyes, just as suspicious as her father was when someone offers something he wants. "Yeah, I want you to do the show."

"Then she comes with me," she says, gesturing to the little girl who hovers behind her. "That's the deal. You take us both or not at all."

As if I was going to leave her for even a second.

She must have believed the bluster I was feeding her father.

I wouldn't leave her, and despite my general lack of interest toward the plight of random children, I probably wouldn't have left that little squirt either.

"Then pack your shit," I say. "Vlad will escort you. I'll stay here. Have a little conversation with your father until you're ready to go. You have five minutes."

She gestures the little girl out of the trailer.

Then she pauses and looks back at her father where he lies in a broken heap.

"Don't," she says.

"You're not going to defend him, are you?"

"No, but he's still my father. Don't kill him."

I nod. I wasn't planning on killing him anyway, mostly because it would attract too much notice. They wouldn't be able to hide such a death from the authorities since the circus would crumble. Someone would call and then they would know to come after us. I'm not going to kill him, but I'm definitely going to beat him up a bit, make him feel a little pain for all the pain he laid down on his daughter. "I promise," I say, and it's so strange that when I speak to her, it always feels like I'm telling the truth.

Chapter Seven

Luna

It takes longer than five minutes.

I hope Emerson doesn't go too hard on my dad, but I need longer.

If I'm really going to be saying goodbye to the circus, not out of sentimentality, out of duty because I have been running the circus for my father for years. I'm willing to leave it all behind for Seraphina, for her to finally be safe and free of him.

It's not even a hard decision.

I've done this all for her in the first place, and this opportunity will be better for her. At least, I hope it will be. It's easy enough to throw all of my clothes, including my performance outfits, my leotards, my tights, along with toiletries into a duffel bag.

They're all jumbled up, not clean, not neat, but it doesn't matter.

I'll sort it out later.

A second duffel bag is slightly more organized with Seraphina's clothes.

One benefit to living in tiny trailers is that we don't actually have a lot of stuff. She packs her own books into her backpack, making it far too heavy for her to actually carry on her small frame.

She doesn't question me.

The poor girl is used to high-stress situations.

Ones where we keep our head down and work in order to survive.

This one is different from the ones we've had before, but she still knows the drill. We move first, take action first, and then talk it out later when no one else is around. My friend Julie is the one who watches Sera when I'm performing, or working with people on the circus. She helps us pack. She's a little less stoic than Sera or me.

Her eyes get misty because she knows what this means.

She knows there won't be time to decompress and discuss it later because we'll be gone.

"You can come with us," I say. "I'm sure he'll take you."

She shakes her head. "My family is here. My cousins." A rough laugh, that familiar burr that comes from smoking for thirty plus years. "Even my ex-husband is here. This is family."

"Whatever happens," I say, a clench in my heart, "we're family too."

Her eyes soften. "I know, sweetheart. This is a fresh start for you, you think I want you to turn it down? You take that little girl and you make your lives better. You don't need me dragging you down."

I bite my lip. "I couldn't have done this without you. You know that, right?"

I'm not talking about tonight. I'm talking about every day, every night. She's the one who held me when I cried as a little girl. She's the one who snuck me food when my father denied me dinner because he didn't like my performance enough. She is the one who actually put a stop to the VIP customers my father would let into my bedroom at night even though my father beat her for it. It never happened again after that night. I owe her so much.

She shakes her head, reading the intention in my eyes. "No, sweetheart, you did it all yourself. I wish that weren't the case. I wish that weren't true. I wish I could have helped you more than I did."

And then I am folded in her thick arms, pressed against her heavy bosom, breathing in the scent of her Virginia Slims. We stay like that for a long moment. Then there's a knock on the door. I know by how hard it was, by the insistence, who it will be before I even open the door.

Emerson Durand, the ringmaster of the infamous Cirque des Miroirs.

Sure, I've heard whispers of him. We all have. He's famous along with Logan Whitmere and Wolfgang as the most successful touring circus in the country, but I don't know anything specifically about him. I don't know anything useful.

I rack my memory for some offhand comment, some piece of gossip, but I have nothing.

Nothing except the overly handsome man standing in front of me, the person who's in charge of my fate. It's a terrifying prospect, but also a hopeful one.

"We're ready," I say breathless.

He leans down and picks up both our duffel bags and Sera's backpack full of books. His eyebrows go up at the weight of it. I know it feels like bricks, but he doesn't falter as he puts it into the SUV. Seraphina and I climb into the back.

I don't know whether to be relieved or not when he enters the other SUV, leaving us with a stranger, a driver who wears sunglasses and doesn't talk to us. Privacy. That's what he's giving us, and I'm grateful for it as Seraphina crawls into my arms. I hold her tight, murmuring a modified version of what happened tonight, a job offer. That's how I spin it, a job offer, as if the gambling debt never occurred. I tell her that we're going somewhere better, somewhere safer.

In turn, she whispers to me about what happened when I was gone, how my father dragged her out of bed, and no matter how hard Julie protested, he would not be denied.

He wanted her to perform, to dance for him.

He wanted to turn her into me.

Another moneymaker for him.

I shiver. I am not going to let that happen. She doesn't have to perform. Not for anyone. I didn't have that choice, but she will. That's a vow I make to myself. I expect us to go to Boise's big airport, but instead we end up at some small airport where we board a private jet.

This is the first big example of Emerson's wealth.

Of Cirque des Miroirs's power.

This is something that my father could never have even considered.

Frankly, we would never even board a plane for any reason, not when we could drive for twelve hours. Or thirty. Here we are on a private jet with bodyguards, or maybe circus members. I don't know. They aren't chatty. They hang out near the front of the plane, near the cockpit, and leave the back for Emerson, me, and Seraphina. She's sitting very stiffly, clearly nervous.

Her little knuckles turned white on the arm of the chair.

"Would you like something to drink?" Emerson asks.

"Water, please," I tell him, not because we're thirsty, but because I think I need alone time with her. She was still partially in shock in the SUV but now her eyes are wide open.

"Of course, ma chère," he says, walking away.

I think he knows we needed a moment because he doesn't immediately grab bottles out of the mini fridge, but instead chats with the man up front.

"Are you okay?" I ask her.

Her wide eyes meet mine, quiet. She's quiet. That's never a good thing. I have learned that when she's a chatterbox, it means she feels safe.

She never chattered around my father.

She only did it around Julie and me. Now she's quiet, even though I'm the only one back here.

"Are you nervous about the plane?" I ask her.

She nods.

"Remember I told you I know how to fly."

Her lips twitch with a smile. "Not like this."

"It's true," I say. "When I'm on my trapeze, I don't go quite as high as a plane, but it's pretty close. Sometimes I wave at them when I'm doing a flip."

She giggles. "No, you don't."

I lean back in my chair, settling in so she can see me being comfortable, and I realize only then that I've been sitting tensely too, that we were probably little mirror images of each other. Even though I have blonde hair and she has dark, I have gray eyes and she has beautiful black, midnight eyes. "The first time I was on a plane, I was scared too," I tell her.

"Where did you go?"

"Remember when Julie told you about the Olympics?"

"You were on the team?" she asks.

I flinch because in a way I was, but also in a way I never was. I never got to experience it. I did all of the work and never got to perform. I nod because I want her to feel safe and comfortable right now. It's not about my past. It's about her future.

"I was nervous, but I had someone to sit with me, someone who had been on plane rides before to tell me that everything would be okay."

"Who was it?"

"It was a coach. Coach Amanda." She was the coach who scouted me. She fought for me, advocated for me, stood up to my father, and it worked all the way up until it didn't.

She still texts me from time to time to check up on me, which is sweet.

Even though it's rude, sometimes I ignore the texts.

Well, that's not quite accurate. I don't ignore the texts. I go back and I look at them and then I turn off my phone and then I open it and look at them and then I turn off my phone again because I have nothing to say. When she asks how I'm doing, I don't know how to tell her that it's not well. I'm not well. I'm not okay but there's nothing anyone can do about it.

Except now the situation has changed, hasn't it? I've left home.

I've left Blue Moon Circus and I'm going somewhere else, beholden to another man. It's not the same thing as being free, but it's close.

She nods. "Are you my coach?"

I smile at her. "Yes, that's exactly what I am."

A frown mars her pretty face. "But I can't fly. Not like you."

Seraphina is afraid of heights. Whether it was because of the stunts my father pulled or something else, I don't know, but she never likes being high off the ground. "That's okay. Your gymnastic tumbles are great in the show, but more importantly, you don't have to be in a show. Not in any show."

She frowns. "I thought we're going to another circus."

"We are, and I'm going to perform, but you'll be able to read your books. Okay?"

"Who will do my school now that Julie's not with us?"

"I'll do it," I tell her, which isn't a lie. I think Cirque des Miroirs has enough money that they don't need me putting up and tearing down tents every day, which means I'll have more time to spend with Sera. It's already a good thing, even if the actual performance is hell. Even if I have to spend the nights in Emerson's bed.

I glance at him.

That's something we haven't talked about again since we saw my father.

He left with his knuckles bloody.

When is he going to come to me again? Where will I sleep? Where will Seraphina sleep? No matter what, I won't let her know that I'm being forced into Emerson's bed for our safety.

Then again, is that really true?

What he did to me in that hotel room felt too good to deny.

He stands there, one of the most handsome men I've ever seen in real life. He looks like he belongs on a movie set. Hell, they probably pay him as much as they would pay some famous actor to be the ringmaster of their circus. Considering they have private jets and huge contracts to buy talent away from other circuses, it makes me wonder why he would need to coerce anyone into his bed when he can already have any woman he wants, probably inside the circus and outside of it.

"Things are going to get better," I tell her. It's a promise that I can't really keep, but that I can't help but make. "You'll see. Things will get better."

She gives me a tremulous smile, trying to be brave for me.

Such a courageous little girl. "Go ahead and sleep."

I stroke my hand through her silky dark hair. Sunlight streams through the jet's windows, but I close the shades. She curls up in her seat. It's a combination of how large and comfortable these chairs are, surely larger than even a first-class cabin would have, and also how small she is that she's able to do it all in one seat without spilling over into mine. Her head rests on her folded hands. In a few minutes, there's a gentle baby snore.

She's used to sleeping whenever she can catch time. Usually when we're driving between cities knowing that she might have to be up again in a moment's notice.

The circus isn't an easy life, but it's ours.

That won't change even if we move circuses.

I throw my jacket over her as a blanket and then stand as Emerson joins me holding two water bottles. I take one and drink deeply, realizing that I'm dehydrated after all this. Hungry too, though my body can't quite process the hunger. There are too many needs, too much excitement, too much adrenaline keeping me full.

"How is she?" he asks, studying her.

"Nervous," I say honestly. "She's nervous."

"And so are you, ma chère."

I nod.

His fingers link through mine, strong and capable, still bloodied from my father, and he tugs me through a door. I'm not sure what I thought was in the door. Maybe a bathroom. Instead, it's an entire room, a room with a bed.

Immediately my muscles go hard and stiff.

I wondered when he would come to me again.

Apparently that time is now.

"Calm yourself," he says. "You won't have to do anything on this bed that you don't enjoy."

I give him a dark look. "I have a feeling that could include a lot of things."

A lazy smile. "You're getting to know me well."

"I'll do anything. Anything. As long as she's kept safe. Understand?"

A shadow crosses his face. "I understand, but you're foolish to give a man complete access for any price. Someone without scruples might take more than you're comfortable giving."

"Do you have any scruples?"

"Not a one."

"That's what I thought."

He grows serious. "I must ask you something. Is she your daughter?"

The question floods my body with ice cold water. Any warmth I felt from our flirting—was that flirting? —evaporates immediately. Is she my daughter? He asks that knowing that I would've just been a teenager when she was born. A teenage pregnancy isn't particularly scandalous in the great scheme of things, except that he also is probably guessing that if she's mine, where she would've come from, who would've been her father.

One of the nameless, faceless men that my dad led into my bedroom when it was dark, they saw me flying through the air and wanted me.

They offered my father money. I don't even know how much.

I never saw a cent, nor did I want to.

"She's not mine," I manage in a hoarse voice.

He closes his eyes, though I'm not sure what he's feeling. Relief. Maybe he didn't want to be with someone who had been a mother before. "I should have killed him," he mutters, and I realize he's angry at my father. Regardless of how that child came to be.

"She's his," I say. "From a woman in a random town. I'm not sure if it was consensual. It definitely wasn't a happy memory for either of them. She didn't know where to find him, didn't have the resources to, but when we passed through town, two years later, she left the baby outside his trailer. I found her one night after a performance."

He swears in French.

My father told me to get rid of her.

That was when I moved into Julie's trailer along with Seraphina.

"I'm the one who named her. Seraphina. Because she reminded me of a little baby angel. And I wanted her to feel safe."

"What about you? Did you want to feel safe?"

"No." I knew that was beyond me.

He looks away. The windows back here have a screen on them so they aren't as bright. Even when they're open, you can see the clouds, the yellows, and the blues without being blinded. I don't know what secrets they have, but he seems intent on them.

"I have a small confession to make," he says, then he faces me. "I don't precisely have an offer from Logan Whitmere."

Shock runs through my body. "What then? Where are we going?"

"Oh, we're going to the Cirque des Miroirs. That's where you're going to work, but I need to prepare you for what's going to happen when we get there."

Dread courses through my body. "Which is what?"

"I may have fallen out of favor with Whitmere."

"Is that code for getting kicked out, getting fired?"

"I suppose you could call it that."

"Oh my God." I can't believe this is happening.

"I behaved badly with the woman he cares about."

My eyes narrow. "Behaved badly, how?"

He makes a negative sound. "Not like that, ma chère. I didn't force her to do anything. I didn't even want her that way, but I feared for the fate of the circus. Our owner was under her thrall. She was a townie playing at being a fortune teller for kicks, which meant he might've settled down with her. He could have left. I caused some problems." There's a pregnant pause illustrating that there's a world of activity behind what happened.

I close my eyes. "So then why are we going there?"

"Logan had his eye on you. He never went after you because he knew that the dollars on the contract wouldn't work, that your father would be pigheaded about it. He, well, I wouldn't say that he is fastidious about morality, but he wouldn't have wanted to take you out of there the way that I did. I saved him the trouble. He's going to accept you."

"And I'm going to be your ticket back into the circus."

"That was the plan," he says, his voice wry.

Christ. Anywhere I go, I'm always someone's meal ticket. First my father's and now Emerson Durand's. "Great. I'm going to sit with Seraphina. Let me know when we get close."

Chapter Eight

Luna

Confusing, frustrating, ridiculously handsome man. I'm going to sit up front and ignore him. Ignore the fact that there's an entire king-sized plush bed back here.

"If that's what you want," he says.

I whirl to face him. "Why wouldn't that be what I want?"

He smirks, a frustrating expression that just makes him look more handsome. "I saw how you looked when you performed. You became far more yourself, less guarded. Free. You love to fly."

"So what?" I ask, unnerved that he could see it. That might sound strange because hundreds of people watch my show every night. They see me fly but they don't see me, they don't see who I am as a person. All they see is my body doing flips.

"I think you'll like what we do up here 30,000 feet in the air."

I scoff. "You would think that. You have all the power here."

It's not the same, which is a silly argument considering I just made that argument to Seraphina. But of course it's not flying on a trapeze. It's freedom.

Whatever happens here in this room, in the back of a private jet, it's the opposite of freedom. It's captivity.

"If you say so," he says, his voice silken. "Then again, if you're interested in power, perhaps I can make a little deal with you."

I give him a dark look. "I'm familiar with your deals. With your bets."

He spreads his hands out wide, and I see in him the ringmaster. "Ladies and gentlemen, come on down to the greatest show on earth."

I roll my eyes but don't interrupt him.

Even in this small space, with a battle looming between us, he captures focus. Even the air pays attention to him. "Luna Rider used her body for other people. Night after night. They've oohed and aahed over her. The great spectacle, the wondrous tricks. *What else can her body do?* She wonders late at night. Perhaps she reaches her hand down to cup her breasts. Or she slides it between her legs."

My cheeks flame. "You're an asshole."

"But tonight, my fair audience," he says, gesturing to the plane windows as if the clouds themselves are watching. "Tonight she's going to experience new heights, powerful heights."

"And cocky."

"And what you may not be expecting is that I, the ringmaster, the announcer, the one who usually stands back and observes, will now become part of the show. You see? I am not going to touch her. She'll touch herself. And I'm certainly not going to hold her down. Or touch her tight little ass. Not unless she asks me to. Not unless she begs."

I roll my eyes. "Unlikely."

"Does she have the courage?" he muses, his dark eyes playful, mysterious. There's a whole world inside those eyes. A land of mystery. No wonder he can lead an entire circus, no wonder he can capture their attention. His body is beautiful, his words are mesmerizing, but even his eyes alone, they could hold me breathless. And they do.

They taunt me, tease me, pull me in.

Until somehow, despite my best efforts, I'm part of this show.

A voice inside me tells me to leave, to close the door, to sit with Seraphina until we arrive. A deeper older part, one filled with primal desires and ancestral wisdom, wants to experience this once. Just once, of my own choosing. And as much as I know I shouldn't trust this man, I at least believe him this far—for the sake of the game. For the sake of the show.

He will follow his own rules not to touch me.

And then, there is that sense of freedom.

My curiosity grows and grows.

Because his cheekbones are so sharp. My fingers have longed for the feel of the trapeze underneath them. In the same way, they now long to feel his cheekbones. And so I allow myself to approach him. I put my right hand up and cup his cheek.

There's bristle. That's a surprise, how sharp it is, like one thousand little knives. Then again, it fits. Those cheekbones should be sharp. They look that way shadowed and angled, beautiful in their brutal handsomeness.

With my palm cupped against his cheek, my thumb rubs gently beneath his eyes. Softly, softly. He holds himself still. He's burning with lust but he doesn't move. He keeps his promise.

"What's next, ringmaster?" I whisper.

"The great Luna Rider needs to understand her equipment, doesn't she? And so she will remove the drapery that's been covering it. She'll look at what she'll be riding tonight."

Rebellion flares inside me. I want to show him that I can see his body without being overcome by lust. It feels like a losing game but I play it anyway, pushing the black jacket off the shoulders, unbuttoning the white dress shirt, revealing a chest that makes my mouth dry.

I've seen plenty of bare chests throughout my life, performers as well as people who work in operations, who pull off their shirts on a hot summer's day as they erect the tents.

Even the men my father would sometimes let into my bedroom.

But I never wanted to touch them. I never reached out and stroked my hand from their neck to their belly button over the valleys of muscles. He curses softly when my hand lingers at the top of his pants, brushing gently at the skin. It's so soft, surprisingly soft.

I thought a man would always be hard everywhere.

Taking off his shirt was already compelling. It already took courage. I'm not sure about the rest. If I undo his pants, won't it be like waving a red flag in front of a bull.

Maybe he wouldn't be able to stop.

On the heels of that thought comes another much more devastating one. Maybe *I* wouldn't be able to stop. Already, there's heat between my legs, a throbbing that wants him there.

"Ladies and gentlemen," he murmurs. "The greatest specimen of its kind, graceful in its simplicity, glorious in its usage. People travel all over the country just to see this."

There's a slight bit of humor in his eyes.

The cockiness gives me the bravery I need to undo his belt.

I tug it from the loops and then swallow hard.

Even through the fabric of his slacks, and when I undo the button and the zipper, I can feel it flex between my fingers, his erection. It makes me nervous but it also gives me power. Isn't that what he offered me? Power.

I push down his boxer briefs and then he's standing there completely nude while I'm still dressed in my performance leotard and loose workout clothes over the top.

"The great Luna Rider," he murmurs. "The best trapeze artist in the world."

Even though this is a game, even though he's just pretending I can't help but feel and flush a little at his words.

"So graceful. So beautiful. So damn talented it takes your breath away. She faces a new apparatus now, something different to hold between those tight little palms."

My breath comes faster. "Is that what you want?" I whisper.

His voice is lower. "I want whatever you have to share."

The words have a ring of truth. They aren't part of the show.

They're just a man speaking to a woman, telling her that her pleasure matters.

I've done a lot of things with my body, a lot of impressive things, but they've always been for other people. Isn't that what he said? They've always been about performing. And this, God, *this*, it's only for me. "Show me," I whisper.

"You will release the lion from its cage? You will allow it to prowl around you, knowing that it might take a bite?"

"Yes," I whisper. "Please."

I thought I wouldn't beg but here I am.

He doesn't fall on me like a ravenous beast. Instead, he circles me, tugging gently, unseen as my light jacket falls to the floor from behind. He reaches around to cup my breasts. They've always been small, and I flush a little but he groans at the sight of his large hands holding my small mounds. I can feel the reaction in his body, the precipice cocked against my ass.

"You're perfect," he murmurs and in that moment it feels true.

He continues undressing me, kissing the places that he finds with light, glancing brushes of his lips, making me shiver despite the cozy warmth of the jet. His kiss when it comes is startling, firm but not quite demanding.

He lets me take the leap.

He's playful. The same way he is as a ringmaster, that's what I think. Calling me in the way he does an audience, allowing me to be part of the show.

I tentatively lick his tongue and he groans his approval.

He pushes me back until I'm on the bed.

And in that familiar position with a man on top of me, it doesn't matter that this man is different, that I chose this. I still freeze. He notices immediately.

Then he turns me so that I'm on top of him, my legs straddling him, his cock heavy between the folds of my sex, my hands on his chest. This way?

"Now watch as the acrobat grasps her new apparatus and positions her body…"

I follow his instructions, mesmerized by his voice, by his eyes, by his body.

My breath catches as I notch the head of his cock at the opening of my body and then slowly, slowly I sink onto him, allowing him to open me fully, crying out at the last inch.

At least I thought it was the last inch.

His teeth grit. He puts his hands on my hips and then thrusts up, going even deeper.

My eyes roll back in my head.

He shows me with his hands, the rhythm. And I ride him.

It's nothing like flying through the air and yet somehow it also is. It's using my body to take risks, to feel exhilarated, to please another person. Though this time, it's not an audience. It's him. It's Emerson, the ringmaster who inadvertently saved me from the nightmare that was my life, who put me on a private jet and brought me to this pinnacle.

He bares his teeth, looking like a lion.

I can't. I can't. I can't get there. Not the way he did it in the hotel room.

Something about it eludes me.

He grasps my hips harder. And then thrust upward. Fast pounding from beneath me.

His strong abs flexing as he does it, and that's what I need, the tiny bit of force, a small bite of pain for me to come. I can feel myself clenching around him. And then he's coming, too, holding back a shout, the veins in his throat pulling tight, his entire body straining as he pauses inside me to climax. And in that moment as I hold myself above him, orgasm singing through my veins, the clouds around me, I know what it means to truly fly.

Chapter Nine

Emerson

Logan Whitmere is the owner of the Cirque des Miroirs.

He, unlike many circus owners, was not born into it, at least not in the traditional sense. He wasn't raised by a circus, but Logan was the son of a performer—a tattooed man. Though he was not that great in person. They put his father behind bars in a freak show that attendees would pay 50 cents to walk through. He wore a loincloth. That was the only piece of clothing he was allowed. While the rest of him was tattooed and etched with color, there were also piercings and a rudimentary form of cartilage injection similar to lip fillers, but they weren't used on his lips. They were used across his body to make the inked mountains and other high points elevate on his skin. In short, he was a freak. A beautiful, terrible freak. Beautiful because there was no denying that his body was art. It was a canvas even more than it was a vessel for a soul. That soul had eroded over time. I'm not sure there would be a way for him to have kept it.

All those people gawking at him night after night, laughing, taunting, throwing things, spitting? At what point did it turn him into a monster? He wasn't truly a captive, just a worker. The bars were there as part of the show, a prop to help the guests feel safe, to taunt him, to show that he was other than human, feral.

After he was done, he could walk around outside with clothes on. He could approach a young woman who lingered at the circus late at night and he could tell her, "Did you see me? Do you want to see the tattoos? Do you want to see the only tattoo, the only part of my body that has a tattoo that no one else can see?"

Whatever was beneath the loincloth, to this day, I have no idea whether he actually was tattooed there. Probably. The circus always favors pain for profit. The very idea of it still makes me and every man around wince. It doesn't seem to matter, though. Because when he had them alone in some private place behind a tent, he did not show them. He held them down. He raped them. It was from that dark legacy that Logan Whitmere was born.

Logan was raised outside the circus. Unlike Luna's little half-sister, his mother kept him, somewhat to her own detriment because small towns are not known to be forgiving of women they deem loose. He only joined the circus as an adult.

I think that's part of what makes him a great leader, though I would never be so gauche as to compliment him to his face. He values safety. He values training. Two things that men like Michael Rider consider unimportant.

They consider them things that just get in the way.

Logan's emphasis on safety has created a great reputation. It makes people want to work for him because he values the talent. The emphasis on training pays off in spades with rave reviews, with viral videos that make people flock to his circus when they barely bother with another.

Of course, every evening spent training is an evening that you can't spend performing.

That's why most owners don't prioritize it.

Logan changed all that.

For one thing, he retired the animals. This was a controversial move since animals are considered part of the circus lore, the circus aesthetic, but it opened up a huge amount of opportunities. We were no longer picketed. We no longer had people trying to block our access.

We became friends with city councils everywhere because we brought money and no drama with protesters. And the animals? Well, the animals got to live here in this large farm in Nebraska where they could retire in peace. By the time Whitmere took over the circus, all of the animals were quite old. They probably did all need to be retired.

Anyway, the elephants lounge or roll around a ball. The tigers enjoy their steak and their heated sauna. It's a great life. It's also home to our training headquarters. We have a separate tent that we use just for training and rehearsals when we're on tour, but during the off-season, we continue to train at the center.

That's where I take Luna.

We arrive with little fanfare, which makes sense because no one is expecting us.

The center isn't only used for retired animals.

It's also used for retired performers.

Circuses tend to chew people up and spit them out.

We use them while they're young and spry, while they perform beautifully, but when they're too old to work physically anymore, they are kicked out. They didn't make enough to save for retirement, which means often they starve or they become the homeless people in random cities that we travel through.

Logan doesn't do that.

Anyone who has been with the circus long enough is available to be transferred to headquarters where they can work on such things like taking care of the retired animals, running the training center, and doing some of the admin and marketing work from afar.

Not only do they not have to flip themselves when they've been injured from decades of work, but they also can live in the same place. There are dorms on site, which is most likely where Luna will stay, but a lot of people also live in the nearby town.

I've never really understood the draw of having a place that is stationary.

If I want a garden, I can get a fucking pot and put it on the windowsill of my high-end, luxury, custom-built RV. Not that I actually want to plant though.

When I look at Luna as she steps off the plane, while she examines the greenery around us and breathes in that crisp mountain air, I start to understand it. Settling down isn't about a place. It's about people. It's about who you settle down with.

I leave the guys behind because I don't want them to get in trouble if this goes south.

And let's be honest, it probably will.

It's something of a pipe dream in the first place, a wild idea. I'm full of wild ideas. It's one of the things that makes me good as a ringmaster, my lack of inhibition.

It's also something that contributed to why I got kicked out of the circus in the first place.

I don't think through my actions.

Well, I'm facing the reality now.

The main building is actually a large ranch house. I knock on the door with Luna and Seraphina in tow, both of them wide-eyed and clearly nervous.

I give them a blinding smile, my ringmaster smile.

It does nothing to soothe them because they're used to people giving performances.

There's a long wait. A small security camera sits at the top of the entranceway. There also would've been security cameras when we drove onto the property, which means there's a real chance that no one ever opens the door. The moment extends.

"Are they expecting you?" Luna whispers.

"Never underestimate the element of surprise," I tell her smoothly.

Seraphina looks at me and then at Luna. Her sister. I suppose I can see it now in the shape of her eye, in the worry that she hasn't quite completely learned how to mask.

"That means no," she whispers to Luna.

The heavy oak panel door swings open, revealing none other than the circus owner himself, Logan Whitmere. He raises an eyebrow at me. That's the only reaction I get to my sudden appearance, but he is all cordiality when it comes to Luna.

"Ms. Rider," he says smoothly. "Please come in, and who is this?"

Luna finds her voice. "This is Seraphina Rider."

To my surprise, Logan crouches down. He's never been what I would call interested in kids. He left that to the clowns, but now he looks genuinely pleased. "Hello, Seraphina. I'm Logan."

She hides behind her sister and then peeks her face out. "Are you an acrobat?"

A faint smile. "Unfortunately, no."

"Me either," she admits, "but I do like to dance as long as my feet are on the ground."

"That's a good rule of thumb," he says, and then he stands.

"Ms. Rider is eager to debut a brand-new show," I say. "One that is sure to be a hit. You already know about her expertise. Trust me when I say it's better than has been advertised.

Before Logan can call me on my bullshit introduction, Seraphina lets out a squeal. "An elephant. *An elephant.*"

Sure enough, as ordinary as if it was a cat or a dog, an elephant wanders past full-length two-story windows at the back of the house. "Can I go see?" she begs.

"I'm not sure," Luna says, biting her lip.

Footsteps come from down the hallway. Sienna Cole has tan skin and dark features, more like Seraphina, the opposite of Luna. She is a beauty, a hard-edged beauty, one that's been tested in fire. A little tan dog trails behind her wearing a puffy collar that looks like it might have started its life as a scrunchie.

This distracts Seraphina utterly from the elephants. She drops to her knees and the dog runs up, making a friend immediately, licking her face until she giggles.

I give Sienna a large, somewhat mocking bow. "I hope you're well, madame."

I don't know why I can't be a regular person, why I can't just say what I mean, why I have to resort to mockery and sarcasm just to interact with people.

She rolls her eyes at me. Then she turns to Seraphina. "If it's okay with your grown-up, I can take you out back and show you which animals are friendly."

Seraphina turns wide eyes on her sister. "Please, please, please, please, *please.*"

Despite the tension of the situation, Luna smiles. "Of course, but remember, don't touch."

"I'll remember," Seraphina says, obviously lying as she cuddles the little dog close to her. Then they're gone, leaving the three of us— Logan, Luna, and I.

"I would have called," I say. "Except then you might have said no."

"I wouldn't ever expect you to listen," Logan says, his voice wry.

Luna steps forward. "I know my arrival here is unexpected, but I can promise you that if you make a place here for me in the circus, I will be a good performer. I also don't mind working outside of performance hours. I don't take up a lot of space and I can help out wherever needed."

Logan shoots me a glance.

We've been friends for years, decades, really, so I know what it means. It means he would like to kick her father's ass. I give him back a look that says already done.

"Ms. Rider," he says, "there is no question that you have a space here in our circus. You are an unparalleled performer. Your reputation precedes you in the best possible way, and Emerson is not given to exaggeration. Well, not when it comes to compliments. If he says you're great, then you're great. You don't have to work outside of your performance hours. All I ask is that you train hard and safely. Does that work for you?"

She nods. "And Seraphina? My sister?"

Logan's expression clears. It's clear he was concerned about the whole possibility of her being Luna's daughter and what it might imply about her misuse.

I will not share the secrets that Luna told me.

No one in this circus needs to know about her past. Not unless she chooses to tell them. "Of course, she can stay with you," he says, "we have tutors on staff, one who travels with us when we go on tour and a couple who stay behind and teach other subjects virtually depending on the child's age. Of course, if you wish to make alternate arrangements for her schooling, that is up to you."

Her eyes are wide. She's clearly never heard of a circus being this helpful to its employees. "That would be incredible. Thank you."

"We also have full benefits for our performers, including health insurance, retirement plans. The training center is also available for people who want to settle down but continue working with the circus. If you were to get injured or just tired of life on the road, you would still have a place with us. We want this to be a place for you to grow safely."

Tears glisten in her gray eyes, making them look like liquid silver.

It wrenches my heart.

"Thank you so much," she whispers.

Logan feigns a casual glance toward the windows where we can see

Sienna showing Seraphina how to pat the trunk of a very old, wizened elephant. "Perhaps you can go with your sister," he says, "and Sienna can give you a tour of the place to get you started. I've already let the staff know that you'll be staying here for tonight. I'll inform them that you're to be given more permanent rooms."

Luna meets my eyes, as if asking whether she should leave my side, which is a loyalty I didn't expect and certainly don't deserve.

I nod. "Go ahead."

She heads toward the door that Sienna left from, but she still pauses to look back at me.

I'll always remember how she looks framed by the sunlight.

It's almost a physical thing surrounding her effervescence. She's so fucking real, real and strong and courageous. Does she know how brave she is? Someone will tell her eventually.

It won't be me.

And then she's gone, leaving me with one of my oldest friends and also my enemy all rolled into one. "I should kick you out of here," he says. "Or at the very least, kick your ass."

"You could try," I say, my tone languid.

His dark gaze flickers to my knuckles, which are still swollen and bloodied from her father, even though I washed my hands. "It looks like you've been fighting recently."

"He didn't want to give her up."

"Can you blame him?" he asks, his gaze too fucking perceptive.

I look through the window. Seraphina's eyes light up when she sees her sister. Sienna's pointing at things, introducing her, showing her around. Soon this will be home base. A comfortable place where she knows she and her sister will always be safe.

"She really is that good," I say, just in case there's any doubt. "A star."

Logan sighs and runs a hand over his face. "Listen."

"Don't.

He goes there anyway. "What you did was fucked up, but you also helped us recover." Then he says the words that I've been longing to hear. "You can come back to the circus."

I can come back to the circus, to home, to the only place that I've ever remotely belonged. I stroll away from him. There's a painting on the wall of the big top, its red flags unfurled, a storm blowing in behind it.

"How did you do it?" I ask. "How did you move on from the past?"

His voice comes from behind me. "How do you know I did?"

"Those tattoos, for one thing." You can see them peeking out from his white shirt sleeves and above the white collared shirts he wears. Sometimes when it's summer and he's helping us put up tents, he'll take off his shirt and I can see all of the colors he's put on his body in defiance of who his father was.

He snorts. "These tattoos, they weren't about healing. They weren't about recovery. They were an experiment to see how far I could go, how deep I could become him before I actually became the monster that he was."

I glance back. "You never even got close."

"I wasn't going to be my father," he says, "but I also wasn't going to be anybody else. Not until I met Sienna. That's the day I started living. The day I became me."

My throat grows dry. "I'm sorry I interfered."

"I know," he says, "because believe it or not, we're friends."

I snort, incredulous. "I doubt Sienna would like that."

"That's where you're wrong. Sienna was the first one to suggest I take you back. I was more protective of her, defensive, I suppose. She's too important to me not to be, but she's also generous, forgiving, and she understands how people can act when they're reacting out of fear."

I narrow my eyes. "I wasn't afraid."

"You're not afraid of anything," he says, faintly mocking.

"We don't choose this life because it's easy." I gesture to the painting. A storm is always a danger to a circus. It doesn't matter how strong our tents or how secure our RVs, something will be destroyed. Someone might get hurt. We battle the elements, mother nature itself.

"You didn't choose this life at all," Logan says.

I absorb the words like they're a blow straight to the gut with a heavy fist.

Didn't I? Unlike Logan, I was born into the circus, raised this way.

I have that in common with Luna.

My mother was an acclaimed equestrian vaulter, the best in the country. If you've never seen it before, equestrian vaulting is basically like doing gymnastics while a horse rides around beneath you. Handstands. Flips. All of it is fair game.

One evening a townie seduced her.

She went willingly, as far as I can tell.

Though she didn't know what would happen next.

She didn't know she would end up pregnant.

It didn't even matter that the poor bastard was willing to send a little money to us on the road. When she told him about me, all that mattered is that her body was never the same. The scars, the weight, those changes might be subtle to most people, but they were enough that she couldn't balance the way she used to.

She couldn't flip, couldn't move as quickly, and one day in a crucial moment, the horse threw her. She was paralyzed.

That's when I went to work.

Not exactly true. I had done odd jobs around the circus my whole life, but it was when I was twelve years old that I became the breadwinner of our tiny family. She lived out her remaining years in a mediocre assisted living facility, paid for by me.

So I guess Logan is right.

It was never really a choice.

A choice implies that there was another option, that there was ever anything else I could do with my life. In the end, the circus is all I've ever wanted, the only place I've ever wanted to be, but we both know it's not what I deserve.

Chapter Ten

Luna

My heart slows down in the moments before a performance.

Every second seems to last an hour.

This time there's no tiger performing for the crowd. There aren't even stands filled with people who bought tickets. There are just other performers, people who were practicing already.

Sienna has a cool mien. I would normally be intimidated by someone like her but she's actually so welcoming and sweet as she walks me through here to show me the equipment. I am so enamored of the beautiful new rigs and setups, nothing torn or rusted.

I look at them longingly, my fingers itching to grip the bars.

My body wanting to fly.

She knows. "You can go up if you want to."

"I would love to," I say, barely able to contain myself.

Seraphina claps. She loves watching me practice.

It's only as I'm standing here, climbing up on a ladder, only about 15 feet off the ground with a trapeze tied up near me that I realize that the other performers, who don't know me from Adam, have stopped their practice in order to watch me.

This might make me nervous.

But the truth is, as soon as I have the bar in my grip, I lose all sight of them, it only becomes about the lift, the flips, the movement. It becomes about flying.

I take hold of the trapeze and then I soar.

It's not my regular performance that I give. It's much more casual than that, much more playful. I'm not doing my most daring tricks, though. I don't know the space and the placement. So, it's a little more limited. But that also gives me a kind of freedom. I can move my body however feels natural.

I'm not trying to impress. I'm just trying to experience these bars. They're experiencing me back. If I'm going to be practicing, rehearsing and working at the circus, we're going to get to know each other very well.

And this…this is like a first date.

A first date equivalent where I'm giggling and he's grinning, and we're getting along perfectly. A first date where we're already falling in love.

I'm not sure how many minutes pass with me in the air.

Enough so that when I land, nailing the landing, a perfect 10—I can know all of that in my head without feeling cocky about it—everyone claps.

Sienna is there, Seraphina is jumping up and down.

Even Logan Whitmere is there, his eyebrows raised, looking impressed. Damn. Maybe I should have thrown in more of my most dangerous stunts if the owner is going to be watching me. He doesn't look disappointed, though.

I try to be subtle about it, but I can't help looking around wondering where Emerson is.

Does he not even care now that I'm in the circus? I was just his meal ticket after all.

Maybe he's already flying off in his private jet somewhere else.

Or he's hooking up with one of the other people who work at the circus here.

That thought sours my stomach.

I walk over to Logan as Sienna shows Seraphina some tumbling mats she can use. She immediately starts rolling around like one of those little roly poly bugs. She does love to roll, she just doesn't love heights.

"That was incredible," Logan says, "especially considering you weren't accustomed to this equipment."

"It doesn't take much to get accustomed to it. Everything works beautifully."

"Keeping our equipment in top shape is important," he says, his expression serious and grave. "It's part of how we keep everyone safe."

Safety. The word sinks into my skin, for once seeming like it might be possible.

I was almost afraid to hope for that.

Not just safety on the trapeze. But safety everywhere. Safety without a man who goes on rampages when he doesn't get his way. Or when ticket sales are too low.

Logan doesn't seem like that.

I didn't really believe Emerson when he talked about him, but I think it's true.

If so, there's no better place for Seraphina.

And I guess… there's no better place for me.

I've been living so long trying to protect her. Trying to protect myself, trying to protect everyone in that circus that I lost sight of the fact that I am worth protecting.

Emerson showed me that.

"Where is Emerson?" I ask.

Logan gives me an odd look. "He didn't say goodbye, I assume?"

My blood runs cold. "Where's he going?"

He sighs. "I probably shouldn't be telling you this."

I cringe, expecting it to be about some woman, some conquest. A person who he's actually interested in aside from the new performer he gambled into his bed. "Please. I want to know."

"He's leaving the circus for good."

Every muscle in my body pulls tight. "What do you mean?" Then realization hits me. "You told him to leave. I wasn't enough to buy his way back into Cirque des Miroirs."

He shakes his head. "No, you are more than enough to gain him entrance back into the circus. The truth is that even without you we might have eventually called him back to us. But he left so that you could have the circus, so that it could be a better place."

I frown. "What do you mean?"

"He doesn't think he's worthy of what the circus has become. He thinks he's a man just like your father."

Surprise already has me shaking my head. "He's nothing like my father."

"I never met Michael Rider but his reputation wasn't good. Unfortunately, Emerson has always believed he embodied the worst of the circus. That he was the dark to my light."

"But that wasn't true. Was it?"

"Did he ever tell you how I came to own the circus?"

I shake my head. I hadn't really put too much question into it.

There was some news about it when I was younger, but I was too little to really pay attention and there's always drama in circuses.

"The previous owner was hurting someone, a woman. I protected her, put myself at risk. I was relatively new to the circus. A townie, as we say. I thought that moment would be the death of me. Emerson was the one who stepped up. He defended her. He defended me. And that is the night we took over the circus."

My eyes widen. He did that. In a way it's a surprise. But also in a way it's not. He didn't simply protect me and Seraphina, didn't take us away. He took us under the auspices of a gamble.

A poker game.

I have a feeling there's no way he would have left that place without us, using whatever means possible. Money. Threats. Violence. He wasn't going to let us be hurt there.

It runs to the very heart of him.

"Please," I say. "Where is he?" I have to see him.

He shakes his head. "He might already be gone. But if he's still here, he's in the residences. He never officially packed up his room here."

All he has to do is point me in the right direction and then I'm off, sprinting, my muscles pumping, my breath sawing in and out of my mouth. There's no athleticism in the way I run right now. Only desperation.

I get another set of directions only once from someone who's passing me in the hall, their eyes wide at the sight of this wild person sprinting. I skid to a halt in front of a room that's massive, the door open revealing a large space big enough for a king-sized bed. A large wooden desk. An actual sitting area with a fireplace.

Emerson is packing a black piece of luggage that's on an armchair.

It's only a carry-on size. People in the circus always travel light.

The room looks bare, despite its beautiful furnishings. Despite the decoration. It could be a room that belongs to anyone. Did he never settle in after all these years? Did he never feel at home?

"What are you doing?" I ask, breathless.

He scowls at me. "Me? What are *you* doing? This is my room. Shouldn't you be out meeting everyone or more importantly the animals?"

"They aren't even in the circus. And apparently neither are you."

He turns away. "Did Logan tell you that? He shouldn't have."

"Were you not even going to say goodbye?"

"No," he says, his voice bitter. "I did not particularly want to see the relief in your eyes. That you would not be in my bed each night."

"You don't want me anymore?"

"I want you too much. That's the problem. I want you so much that I took you and I made you mine. That I did the same thing those men did who paid your father. I used you just like them, and that's why I have to leave you alone."

The words are like an electric shock for my system.

They wake parts of me that were long dormant. The womanly parts. The grown-up parts that never knew I could even long to belong to someone.

"What if I want to be yours?"

He waves his hand. "You'll find someone else. Some handsome all-American trapeze artist who can pair with you, who's your age. Who wants to start a sweet little family."

I narrow my eyes. "So that's it. You're just giving up."

He snarls. "Don't you know how hard this is? I'm leaving so you can have a better life, so that you can have the circus as it should be, unencumbered by me."

"You think you're going to weigh me down?"

"Of course I will. I'm a fucking stone around your neck."

I close the door behind me, locking us both inside. "I look at it a little differently," I say, strolling into the room, finding some of his charm, some of his insouciance. "My father is the one who taught me to walk on a tightrope. He forced me to do it until I bled."

Emerson makes a growling sound.

"He didn't want me to go away. All he wanted was the money, the money that I could bring him whether I was an act in the circus, or whether I was making sponsor deals with brands. It was only when he realized that if I truly left, if I made something of myself and didn't perform in the circus, if I meddled, I would have resources that would go beyond him. I would be able to leave. And he didn't want that. He used me, Emerson."

"Just like I used you," he says. "I used you as my ticket back into the circus."

I make a humming sound. "No, you didn't. Because you're leaving."

He lets out a harsh breath.

"Why?" I whisper. "Why aren't you staying?"

"Because I can't do it. I can't be like your father. I can't use you as my ticket to get what I want. You belong here. You belong in this circus where you can be free. And safe. That's my gift to you."

"Thank you," I say, taking a step closer.

"I don't want your fucking gratitude."

"Too bad. You're going to get it." I pull off my tank top, revealing a sports bra. There's not much up here. But it seems to work for Emerson.

His dark gaze narrows. His nostrils flare. That handsome face turns into a snarl of desire. "What are you doing?" he asks, his voice hoarse.

I step forward and kiss him.

At first he doesn't move. Even as I press my lips against his.

Only when I nip his bottom lip does he react, grabbing me close, feeling me everywhere. My ass. My thighs. My breasts. He kisses me so hard I can barely breathe, and I love it.

"What are you doing?" he asks again.

There's less defiance now, more surrender.

As if he won't be able to leave.

I smile against his lips. "What I do best, but a little different. This time I'm doing it the way you taught me… I'm going to fly."

* * * *

Also from 1001 Dark Nights and Skye Warren, discover Behind Closed Doors, Finale, and The Bishop.

Sign up for the 1001 Dark Nights Newsletter
and be entered to win a Tiffany Key necklace.

There's a contest every month!

Go to www.1001DarkNights.com to subscribe.

**As a bonus, all subscribers can download
FIVE FREE exclusive books!**

Discover 1001 Dark Nights Collection Eleven

DRAGON KISS by Donna Grant
A Dragon Kings Novella

THE WILD CARD by Dylan Allen
A Rivers Wilde Novella

ROCK CHICK REMATCH by Kristen Ashley
A Rock Chick Novella

JUST ONE SUMMER by Carly Phillips
A Dirty Dare Series Novella

HAPPILY EVER MAYBE by Carrie Ann Ryan
A Montgomery Ink Legacy Novella

BLUE MOON by Skye Warren
A Cirque des Moroirs Novella

A VAMPIRE'S MATE by Rebecca Zanetti
A Dark Protectors/Rebels Novella

LOVE HAZARD by Rachel Van Dyken

BRODIE by Aurora Rose Reynolds
An Until Her Novella

THE BODYGUARD AND THE BOMBSHELL by Lexi Blake
A Masters and Mercenaries: New Recruits Novella

THE SUBSTITUTE by Kristen Proby
A Single in Seattle Novella

CRAVED BY YOU by J. Kenner
A Stark Security Novella

GRAVEYARD DOG by Darynda Jones
A Charley Davidson Novella

A CHRISTMAS AUCTION by Audrey Carlan
A Marriage Auction Novella

THE GHOST OF A CHANCE by Heather Graham
A Krewe of Hunters Novella

Also from Blue Box Press

LEGACY OF TEMPTATION by Larissa Ione
A Demonica Birthright Novel

VISIONS OF FLESH AND BLOOD by Jennifer L. Armentrout and
Ravyn Salvador
A Blood & Ash and Fire & Flesh Compendium

FORGETTING TO REMEMBER by M.J. Rose

TOUCH ME by J. Kenner
A Stark International Novella

BORN OF BLOOD AND ASH by Jennifer L. Armentrout
A Flesh and Fire Novel

MY ROYAL SHOWMANCE by Lexi Blake
A Park Avenue Promise Novel

SAPPHIRE DAWN by Christopher Rice writing as C. Travis Rice
A Sapphire Cove Novel

EMBRACING THE CHANGE by Kristen Ashley
A River Rain Novel

Discover More Skye Warren

Behind Closed Doors
A Rochester Novella

Marjorie Dunn is hiding in plain sight. The past can't find her at the peaceful inn she owns in a quiet coastal town in Maine.

Until Sam Brewer walks through the door. He arrives in the dead of night, with a dark suit and storm-gray eyes.

Marjorie knows better than to trust this stranger, but she can't resist his touch. Every kiss binds them together. Every night draws the danger close.

She risks her heart with him, but more than that, she risks her life.

The past has caught up with her. And it wants her dead.

* * * *

The Bishop
A Tanglewood Novella

A million dollar chess piece goes missing hours before the auction.

Anders Sorenson will do anything to get it back. His family name and fortune rests on finding two inches of medieval ivory. Instead he finds an injured woman with terrible secrets.

He isn't letting her go until she helps him find the piece. But there's more at stake in this strategic game of lust and danger. When she confesses everything, he might lose more than his future. He might lose his heart.

* * * *

Finale
A North Security Novella

Francisco Castille, the exiled Duke of Linares, knows his duty. Even in modern times, the line must continue. So he'll marry and produce an heir.

Yes, a wife will fit into his well-ordered life.

Instead he ends up with the brilliant pianist Isabella. Strong. Spirited. And highly disobedient. She rebels against every custom and every rule, threatening his careful balance.

Francisco never backs away from a challenge.

Isabella never bows down to anyone.

This scorching hot battle of wills may leave both of them broken.

About Skye Warren

Skye Warren is the New York Times bestselling author of dangerous romance. Her books have sold over one million copies. She makes her home in Texas with her loving family, sweet dogs, and evil cat.

For more information, visit https://www.skyewarren.com.

On Behalf of 1001 Dark Nights,

Liz Berry, M.J. Rose, and Jillian Stein would like to thank ~

Steve Berry
Doug Scofield
Benjamin Stein
Kim Guidroz
Chelle Olson
Tanaka Kangara
Asha Hossain
Chris Graham
Jessica Saunders
Stacey Tardif
Dylan Stockton
Kate Boggs
Richard Blake
and Simon Lipskar

Made in the USA
Middletown, DE
20 March 2024